Quest of the Dreamer

Dragons Vs. Drones Book 1

Brett Monk, Lace Brunsden

Big Why Media

Contents

Forward by Brett Monk 1

1. Chapter 1 2

2. Chapter 2 7

3. Chapter 3 13

4. Chapter 4 21

5. Chapter 5 30

6. Chapter 6 43

7. Chapter 7 54

8. Chapter 8 61

9. Chapter 9 73

10. Chapter 10 87

11. Chapter 11 99

12. Chapter 12 112

13. Chapter 13 117

14. Chapter 14 124

15. Chapter 15 137

16. Chapter 16 148

17. Chapter 17 156

Afterword 160

About the Authors 161

Forward by Brett Monk

Welcome to the world of Alyrraesia and the epic tale of Dragons Vs. Drones!

Lace and I are working hard (and having so much fun) creating a family-friendly epic sci-fi fantasy, and we hope you thoroughly enjoy it.

You'll notice references to an event known as "The Great Change" which had a profound effect on this world. While the novels will tell you more and more about that event as we go along, there's a special novella called "The Great Change" that you can receive and read for free at this link.

https://www.brettmonk.com/community

When you join the community, you will not only get free books and other content by me and some of my friends, but you will get the inside scoop on discounted products and upcoming releases. Plus, I share some personal thoughts and "behind the scenes" photos and notes about my life, media adventures, and favorite grilling recipes. :-)

Community members also get to vote in polls and make suggestions for upcoming books and projects. You might even want to consider being a "beta reader" or an "advance review reader", both of whom get to read the books before they're available to the public!

More details are available at this link: https://www.brettmonk.com/community

Chapter 1

The prince hadn't had a good night's sleep for weeks. That was worrisome enough by its own merit. But if his fears were correct, after tonight he would be unlikely to rest for a long time to come. He paced around his chamber, the single flickering candle adding a morsel of warmth and movement to the cold blue shaft of moonlight that pierced the room from the window above, giving his bed a ghostly glow.

The last time the "Dreamer's Moon" appeared was many years ago, just before his mother died. Just before so many other things became bleak and sour. He tried to think, to plan what to do next if tonight turned out to be like that night. It was the dizzying confusion of what might happen next that finally numbed his exhausted brain enough to place his head on the pillow.

The first thing that happened as he did so was that his room, and the high tower that held it, fell away leaving only him and his bed suspended in the sky. He jolted up and tried to cling to the bed for safety, but his cot, blanket, and pillow all dissolved and melted away like spun sugar thrown into a pot of boiling water. He closed his eyes to anticipate falling to his death. But the sensation of falling did not come.

When he opened his eyes, he was someplace else. That was when he knew for sure his fears had been fulfilled. He was having a vision.

As he looked around, thunder of marching feet and the clash of steel on steel cascaded over the scorched battlefield. War cries and death screams rang out in some languages he recognized, and others that he did not. Deep roars, high-pitched whines, and blasts of intense heat pressed down from overhead. The clamor reverberated through Myrddin's chest. He could barely breathe through the stench of singed flesh and melting metal, constantly dodging the flames and falling debris from the sky above.

He was surrounded by monsters he had only heard of in campfire tales from grizzled warriors. They were crafted of metal thinner than chainmail, with glowing eyes which stared into your soul, though they clearly had none of their own. They were lifeless, yet skilled and efficient at taking the lives of the creatures they encountered. The pounding of their march was as steady as a heartbeat, but with an unnatural clockwork timing which made it practically hypnotic.

Some of the killing machines bore a humanoid physique. Others were shaped unlike any breathing creature in Alyrraesia. There were grotesque monstrosities with spinning blades pointing in every direction. Others could issue a beam of crimson light which cut through flesh like a fiery sword. Still others carried cannon of different sizes and shapes, firing small balls of metal faster than an arrow or a thrown axe, ripping through the skin and armor of their organic opponents.

A loud explosion, followed by a high whine, rang above Myrddin's head and grew louder rapidly. As he glanced upward, he saw a flaming, spinning metal object plummeting from the sky and heading toward him. He dove headlong forward as it crashed where he had stood. As he lay on the ground, a giant dragon swooped barely over him, making sure the machine at his feet had been destroyed. The gust of wind from the mighty beast's wings almost flattened the elf.

Laying on his back, he scanned the battle in the sky above. As he and the other land bound races fought against the walking and rolling death machines, the mighty dragons waged war with the drones. They were as deadly and unrelenting as the robots but had the added advantage of flight. Not the elegant, forward flowing flight of a bird, but a jerky, unnatural flight which allowed them to hover in a single place, and even to travel backwards to attack or retreat.

All around him, he recognized different races; dwarves, centaurs, dryads, even MoleKind. But he was the only elf. There were fewer of the living creatures than robots, and their numbers declined as each minute passed. Even with the support of the dragons, which was rare these days, they would not win the battle

But he continued to fight, swinging his sword in every direction, inflicting as much damage as he could.

A dwarf drew up alongside Myrddin, the sturdy warrior's bright red hair and beard catching his attention. He swung a massive hammer around in circles, sometimes merely glancing off the machines, other times managing to find a spot weak enough to make a dent, or occasionally a crushing blow.

The harsh clang of metal reverberated through the air with every strike of the dwarf's hammer, sending a shiver down the prince's spine. The dwarf appeared to be gaining the advantage, as the metal beast took a step back from the hammer blows. Then, with a grinding sound, a cavity on its shoulder opened, revealing a tube loaded with a metal projectile.

Before the dwarf could retreat or dodge the attack, the projectile launched from the tube, trailing a tail of smoke and flame in its wake. As if in slow motion, the prince watched the missile impact into the dwarf's chain mail. At first, it appeared that the armor and the thick skin of the dwarf would simply be pushed back by the flying weapon.

Then came the explosion. The harsh sound of clanging metal was replaced by the sound of ripping flesh, the feel of a small splatter of blood against the prince's face, and the sensation of being vaulted through the air by the impact.

As a trained warrior, Myrddin tried to roll with the blow as he hit the ground, but was halted by searing pain. He glanced down to find a shard of metal had found a gap in his armor, ripping through the flesh within.

While he had been spared a few moments, his reality sunk in.

He was going to die.

Another machine advanced upon him, the heavy steps of its march reverberating through the ground. He felt his sword leaving his hands as they lost their strength along with the rest of his body. Myrddin could not protect himself.

A panel on the robot's chest slid open and several arms extended, with blades spinning and twisting in every direction. It came straight for Myrddin, and he had barely enough time to turn his body and watch as the creature bent down, the blades reaching for his head.

He was going to die.

Myrddin woke with a start. The elven prince, who was bracing himself to feel the robot's blades tearing through his body, suddenly found himself safe in the comforts of his bed, shivering and covered in sweat. The shaft of moonlight had passed from his bed and now lit his bookshelf on wall beside him.

For a moment, he was too shocked to realize what was had happened and let out a gasp of fear. Thankfully, there was nobody to hear it. He had been dreaming. He was safe. At least for now.

He rose slowly, his heart pounding in his chest, the blood rushing through his ears reminding him of the sounds of the robotic feet hitting the ground. Myrddin stared at the moonlit books on the shelf and took a deep breath. He tried to project his thoughts into happy memories of reading tales of adventure or receiving praise from his tutors for his academic skills. His body continued to shake for several long moments, but he finally calmed himself enough to stand.

Myrddin had had similar vivid dreams before. The most notable, years ago, was not of a battle, but of the death of his mother. The feeling was the same, however, and he knew what had happened directly afterwards. She had died, exactly as he had seen it in the dream. Every detail had played out as he had foreseen in his sleep.

As a child, he had told the elders and leaders every detail. He had told them that the headaches she complained of were more serious than just "tiredness". He had told them that if she didn't leave the royal city and seek the help of the Dryad healers that she would die in great suffering.

He could still remember her screams in her final days as the madness set in for the last time.

The elders ignored the foolish nightmares of the child, and even after the event occurred, most of them dismissed his dream as coincidence. But the story of his premonition spread among the common folk, and the prophetic dreams of the elf prince became a legend which vexed officials of the royal court to this day.

He rose and started preparing himself for a meeting with the council of the Elven elders, and with his father, the king. Myrddin scanned his room to consider his wardrobe for the meeting. Having been ostracized his whole life by his father and the advisors, he'd been in the habit of deliberately dressing in a common tunic rather than the finery of the court. But today he had an important message to deliver, and the appearance of a petulant youngster would not suit his mission.

He gazed at the tub of icy water in the corner of his room, still there from the evening before when he had cleaned himself before getting into bed. It did not look nearly as appealing now, but he got in anyway, gritting his teeth against the icy chill as he did so.

The icy waters of the bath only exacerbated the tremors still sweeping through his body. In his mind, he rehearsed how he expected the presentation to go, including the inevitable reactions of disdain from the king. While he had tried over the years to get used to the constant disapproval, it never ceased to sting. It wasn't his fault his older sister had died so tragically. Mostly because he hadn't yet been born. But after her death and all the destruction afterward, his father had put her memory on a pedestal too high for Myrddin to ever measure up to.

As he sat in the freezing water, he realized his own heart longed for the sister he never knew. The sister who had died almost a thousand years before. But she was not there to help him, and so he did what he had to, and prepared himself as well as he could. He would have to deal with this either way. He might as well do it properly.

When he finally emerged from the bath, he dried himself thoroughly before combing out his long hair and dressing in his finest clothing. It was not the glorious robes of the days before, but given the circumstances, they would have to do.

His sister had been alive in a time of plenty when she would have been able to wear beautiful crowns and dresses every day without having to worry about much. She would have been able to bathe daily, and in warm water too. Prince Myrddin did not have the luxuries of his dead sister.

His simple tunic had once been a fine piece of clothing made of pale, white cotton of the highest quality. It had frayed in multiple places, having been worn for many years without repair. He stared at the hem, where the fraying was the most visible, making sure to tuck it neatly into his trousers so it would not be visible to the courtiers.

His trousers were in a similar condition. The best item of clothing he had, by far, was his boots. They were simple, but of good quality leather, treated by both the dwarves and the elves to create a masterpiece. The heels and toes were all scuffed, but still intact, and showed no signs of giving out anytime soon.

It was not that he minded having older items of clothing, or even the little room, with a simple bed and tattered blanket all the elves of that time had to put up with. What he did mind was the fact that it was different from what it used to be, and nobody seemed to care.

They would not have much choice soon, though. If his dream was correct, then they would have to do something, or they would risk their entire species dying out. Myrddin could not allow that, but he was not so sure about the king.

With one last look at himself in the mirror, he was pleased to see he at least looked clean and neat, and with that, he went off to meet the king and his council.

Chapter 2

The prince descended the winding stairs of the tower from his chamber. He had insisted on staying in the room he had grown up in, even after his father ordered everyone to move deeper into the heart of the castle. His father, usually quick to confront any rebellious decision, or any decision he made, didn't say a word.

He passed several elves in the dimly lit hallways of Killiad, the ancestral home of the elves. The hour was still early, but since the population had retreated into the heart of the castle, where sunlight was scarce, they did not have regular sleep schedules. Elves might be found going about their business at any hour. But their numbers were few, and the prince politely dodged them without drawing attention. He moved as quickly as possible without appearing to be alarmed. The people already lived in fear of extermination and the appearance of concern from the prince would only inflame their concerns.

Since his childhood, tutors had taught him how the Elf Kingdom had been before the Great Change, the day the machines came to life and the rest of the world started dying. Thousands of elves, working, singing, and laughing in the sun, enjoying life. Now, there was only a dwindling remnant, hidden away, trying desperately to survive. Every time he passed another elf, he smiled as genuinely as possible, trying to set his own worries aside.

He strode deeper and deeper into the darkness of the castle to reach the council room. His father, King Dalen, had withdrawn from the outside world some time ago and had taken the other elves in leadership positions with him. Other elves would sometimes emerge from the depths of the castle to complete their tasks, but the king never did. So, to visit him, the prince would have to go there.

The prince finally reached the heavy wooden doors of what now served as the royal court. He tried unsuccessfully to hold back an expression of disgust as he stared at the gloomy corridor around him. The room appeared to have been used for storage a long time ago, perhaps to keep grains cool and dry during the wet summer months. Now it was being used as the court of the mighty king, a king who looked upon him as a failure.

He shook off the self-indulgence and prepared to enter the room. He straightened out his clothing and ran his hands over his hair to tame any wild strands. And then he raised his hand and knocked.

And waited.

His frustration grew, but he knew better than to enter the room without the approval of whoever was inside with his father. He had only done so once as a child and had no desire to repeat that event.

Eventually, the door opened and the head of one of the king's favorite advisors emerged. At the sight of the prince, the dark-haired elf's eyes widened in shock. He withdrew into the room, presumably to announce Myrddin's presence. Seconds later, the doors swung open, and he was ushered into the room with a bow from the advisor.

The flickering wall torches and the two candelabras on each side of the king gave the room just enough light to discern faces. Myrddin was relieved that most of the council was present. He would only have to relay his message once, and the one or two members who were absent would learn the news soon enough.

The members of the council all sat around an oval table which rose to about knee height. They were seated on what must have once been some of the finest cushions in all of Alyrraesia, but now resembled folded blankets after years of being compressed under the weight of the aging elves.

At the opposite end of the table, in clear view of the door, was the king. The remnants of his golden armor which once shone like the sun polished to perfection daily, now sat dully in the dim light, covered in dents and scratches from years of neglect. His cloak, once a brilliant emerald green, was now a dull gray where it hung behind him.

The prince sank to one knee and prepared himself for the vicious onslaught that he expected to follow his statements.

"Father," he said, trying to sound as confident possible while still being respectful of the man before him.

His greeting was met with a disgusted scoff. The prince glanced up to meet the disapproving stare of the man whom he had not laid eyes on in several months.

"Prince Myrddin," the king started scornfully, "you should not speak so casually when you are in this throne room. The people might begin to think you are unsuitable for your position."

The prince resisted the urge to roll his eyes.

"Of course, my apologies to you, my king. I forget myself," Myrddin said, bowing his head lower yet. He noticed he had somehow managed to let a little bit of sarcasm slip into his voice, but hoped it was small enough that the king did not notice.

He did notice though. And narrowed his eyes at the prince.

"What is it that you have come here to speak to us about?" he asked, disgust clear in his voice.

Myrddin paused for a moment, taking a final consideration of how to best phrase his words. He did not want to be too blunt, or he would risk his father shutting him down completely before he had a chance to tell the full tale. But if he took too long, the same would happen.

"I... have had... a vision… in a dream," he started tentatively.

The eyes of the council members grew wide as they shot looks of concern and dread among themselves. Myrddin expected this reaction, after the tragic outcome of the previous dreams he had dared to mention. Their expressions confirmed he had seized their attention. Now he just hoped it would be enough to overcome his father's dismissal long enough for him to speak.

"Another one of your dreams and you wish to speak about it here?" he yawned at the prince without looking at him in the eyes.

The council members were not so dismissive, though. Clearly, they were aware of the reputation the royal advisors had developed the last time they'd ignored one of Myrddin's dreams. After a brief flurry hushed murmurs, one elf cleared his throat and began to speak.

It was the elf directly to the right of his father, Bayard Andorris, the commander of what little remained of the Elven armies. He was also one of the few elves born in the time before the Great Change who was still alive. Bayard was an outstanding warrior and had worked hard to earn his position.

"Your majesty," Bayard started respectfully, "perhaps it would be best to listen to what the prince's dream entailed, after all, we all recall when he previously had a dream which he deemed significant enough to mention to us all."

The rest of the council nodded in agreement with Bayard. While under the current political climate they seldom questioned or challenged the king's decisions, they still maintained enough resolve not to allow an announcement like this to be dismissed without consideration.

Myrddin suppressed a smile of satisfaction.

The king surveyed the room, scrutinizing each face (except Myrddin's) to discern if any had a crack in their resolve. After his attempts to stare down his advisors failed, he stared forward with clenched teeth for what felt like an eternity. He then let out a noise which was somewhere between a sigh and a groan.

With a stiff nod from the king, the prince started his story.

"I was in the midst of a furious battle, fighting alongside creatures of Alyrraesia from many races. Dwarf, Elf, Centaur, MoleKind and others fought side by side on the ground while the mighty dragons soared overhead."

The council members nodded to each other with bright eyes and smiles of hope and satisfaction. Before the Great Change, the magic-bearing races of Alyrraesia had all lived in peace. Some, such as the elves and dwarves, held deep friendships and close alliances. In those days, even the humans were considered tolerable. Everyone dreamed that such days might one day return, but few expected they would live long to see such times.

"But we were losing badly." The prince continued. "The machines had formed themselves into a formidable army. The humanoid robots, spider-machines and other steel monsters wrought destruction on our ground forces while the drones attacked the dragons in the air."

The council's expressions shifted from concern to terror at the thought of an organized army of drones and robots. Until this point, the machines had only attacked in small patrols and raiding parties and had already brought most races to the brink of destruction. The idea of a massive machine army could mean the end of all life on Alyrraesia.

"An army of machines? Are you sure?" asked one of the other elves. He was sitting at the very end of the table, far away from the king. The prince did not remember his name, and his position on the table indicated his inferiority in comparison to the others.

"I am," Myrddin replied solemnly. "How could I not be when the last thing I recall is one of the robots ripping a wound in my chest, possibly killing me."

He knew this would get the attention of those who were not worried yet. The death of the prince and only current heir to the throne was not something they would simply ignore.

"Perhaps," Bayard started, a thoughtful expression in his eyes, "this is something we should consider more seriously, sire. If Prince Myrddin is correct and this doom is coming, then we will not be able to hold off the creatures. We cannot stand up to an army as we are now."

The king appeared to agree with his commander, albeit through increasingly clenched teeth. Looking at the straining jaw muscles on the king's face, Myrddin was amazed his teeth had not shattered yet.

"Agreed!" another elf spoke up. "The most recent count of our population was only at some three hundred elves, and those include the smallest of children who have been born recently. We don't even have fifty able warriors who could fight against such an army."

Bayard nodded in confirmation, "You are correct."

The room was silent for some time. The prince stood in silence, hoping they were all thinking over his words and their consequences carefully.

Finally, it was the king who broke the silence.

"Over the years, our numbers have dwindled until now, where the once-great Elven nation has become insignificant. Perhaps now is not the time for us to fight. There are so few of us, perhaps we need to retreat deeper into the mountains until we have grown strong enough to make a difference."

"Deeper into the mountain?" Myrddin exclaimed, unable to contain himself. "Sire we are not dwarves, our people thrive in the sunlight, amongst the trees, this will only serve to ruin us further."

"Perhaps it will," the king waved his comment off, "but what other choice do we have. If you are so unhappy with this, then perhaps you should take it up with the dwarves. After all, they are one of the reasons why we are all in this predicament to start with."

"That was over a thousand years ago!" Myrddin said indignantly.

"Yet I was alive back then," the king retorted, "and so was your sister."

Myrddin clenched his teeth and swallowed back the bile rising from his stomach. Whenever his father was about to lose an argument, or be held accountable for a poor decision, he would refer to the death of his sister, shutting down any further discussion. This was one of the many reasons he so seldom sought out his company.

"What would Princess Mythria have said about the situation? What would she have recommended you do?" Myrddin asked. Perhaps his voice was firmer than he had meant it to be, but at this point, he had little to lose.

He did not realize the gravity of his words until they had left his mouth. He knew exactly what his sister would have done, what she did do. And everyone in the room knew she had ended up dead because of it.

"Leave me!" the king shouted as he rose suddenly from his position, pointing his finger at the door behind Myrddin.

"But..." the prince started, but he was cut off. He had gone too far, hit too many nerves, and he knew it.

"Leave."

His eyes met Bayard's before he turned. The commander nodded to him with an expression of understanding. He would take care of the king. Without another word, the prince turned and left.

Chapter 3

The prince slipped through the corridors of Killiad as briskly as possible without alerting others to his displeasure. He held back the intense anger bubbling in his chest. He was tempted to run through the halls, shouting at the top of his lungs about how the king was a coward who did not care for his people. But such an outburst would only drive his beleaguered subjects further in despair.

The prince found his way to the outer wall of their mountain fortress and gazed down into the remnants of the old city.

All the young elves had heard stories about the place, about how people once gathered in the streets by the thousands, not only the elves, but also the other races and creatures. Merchants would trade, bards would sing ballads, children would play. Now there was not a soul present.

The buildings, once beautiful, had fallen to ruin due to almost a thousand years of neglect. Only a few crumbling structures and piles of rubble remained.

Not even the birds frequented this place. It was too desolate, too barren. The silence which remained was so deep it seemed to suck the energy out of the air.

He paused to lean on the ornate windowsill of what would have probably once been a busy hallway in a fully functioning castle, as an elf appeared around a corner. He panted as if he had been running and stopped so suddenly the soles of his military boots skidded on the gravel and cobblestone ground.

He appeared to be in a rush, almost as if he had been looking for the prince for quite some time and had taken to running through the corridors. As soon as he recognized the displeasure on the prince's face, the new elf's own features fell.

The young elf went up to his friend and bowed low in deference. Then, with a mischievous gleam in his eye, he rose and slapped Myrddin across the back jovially.

"Wow, you certainly know how to ruin a party!" he exclaimed.

The prince's face brightened as he burst out laughing, "Evakhan, so good to see you, my friend."

The prince took his young friend's hand, shaking it warmly in greeting.

"And you too, my prince," young Evakhan said sarcastically, seemingly purposefully putting his emphasis on the final part of the sentence. He knew full well how the prince disliked being reffered to by his title only.

"Oh, don't you start with me now!" he scolded Evakhan, but his mood was already much brighter than a few moments before.

"How can I not, when you react with such delightful disgust?" Evakhan laughed, the prince joining in.

They stood for a moment, chuckling at one another, looking out over the beautiful green scenery which they so rarely laid their eyes on. They relished the sun on their faces, absorbing as much heat as possible before they had to return to the dreary castle.

Eventually, Evakhan's curiosity overtook him, and the words tumbled out of his mouth.

"Is it true?" he asked. "I mean, you had another dream?"

The prince paused for a second, unsure of what to tell his young friend. Evakhan was so innocent and happy. It would be a sadness to force him into the cold reality. But, as he thought of the gravity of his dream, and the fact that the word had already gotten out, he decided he would serve his friend better my telling him than to keep him in the dark.

"I have. And the dream was troubling."

Evakhan paused as well, his brow furrowed with contemplation.

"You think this one will come true as well." He said as a statement, not a question.

The prince nodded, confirming what Evakhan already knew, "Yes, and I dread the day it does."

The prince could tell his friend longed to ask what the dream was about. His mouth opened and closed slightly as he started to say something, but then changed his mind.

Evakhan understood the prince was protecting him, and Myrddin was grateful his friend did not press the issue.

After a long thoughtful pause, Evakhan asked, "Is there anything I can do to help?"

"No, I don't think so. I don't think there is anything anyone can do. But please promise me if my father drags us all deeper into these mountains, you will stay by my side and keep me sane," he joked, trying to lighten the mood, but he failed. Their faces had grown somber again, even the jovial Evakhan.

The prince observed tears rising in Evakhan's eyes. His friend knew him well enough to discern the gravity of what was said, and what was left unsaid.

He thought of all his other friends, of the female elf he had been considering courting, for the sake of the council and his father. They would not survive going deeper into the mountains. They would shrivel up and die, or perhaps they would turn into horrible creatures, like how the humans had turned into the MoleKind.

"Do you think the elven race will survive?" Evakhan asked. The prince heard the young elf's voice quivering and looked on as tears threatened to spill down his cheeks.

"I don't know. I honestly don't," the prince replied, looking at his dear friend.

Seeing the young elf struggling, he placed his hand on Evakhan's shoulder.

"I look around sometimes and try to remember the time not long after I was born when there were many of us, and we filled the streets out there with laughter and music, but I can't find any trace of it in my mind. Nor any hope of such a future ever being possible for us!" Evakhan ranted.

"I know," Myrddin replied gently. "I try to remember too sometimes, but such memories are too distant."

"What do you think she saw?" The young elf inquired.

The prince bowed his head and closed his eyes. He knew exactly who Evakhan was talking about, and thought for a moment he must have said her name out loud. But he hadn't. Evakhan gave him a sympathetic look. Perhaps he had a tell when he was thinking about her, maybe an expression on his face which his young friend had come to recognize.

The prince replied. "I don't know. But I wish I could have seen this world through her eyes."

They stood for a moment in silence, each contemplating the past, present, and future of their race, themselves, and each other.

Their peace was disturbed by the sound of feet rapidly hitting the stone floors of the corridor, joined by the rapid panting of the owner of the footsteps.

To Myrddin's surprise, it was Bayard Andorris, and he was running towards them quicker than Myrddin had ever seen any elf move outside the battlefield.

"My Prince, My Prince!" he shouted.

Myrddin ran to meet him. The elf was rather old, and the prince did not want him overexerting himself and causing harm.

"General Bayard," he shouted in reply as he neared the elf, "how can I help you?"

He realized Evakhan had followed him and had barely kept up with the prince only when the panting Bayard greeted him as well.

"Prince Myrddin, Elf Evakhan, fresh news has arrived from the centaurs," he paused, looking at the young elf next to the prince before looking back, "For your eyes only."

The young elf nodded, and politely stepped next to Bayard, so Myrddin could view the message in privacy. "For your eyes only?" Evakhan commented, "You mean they wouldn't even let the king see it?"

"No," Bayard said, ducking his head as he handed Myrddin a little piece of thick parchment, rolled so tightly it was thinner than a twig, and no longer than a thumb, "And he is furious. He wanted to destroy the message before I brought it to you."

"I suppose I had better read quickly then," the prince said.

The fact that he was the only one allowed to read it did not mean he could not share the information with those around him. He knew something of how the centaurs worked. Their ways were peculiar and their words were exacting.

The centaurs themselves had certainly delivered the message. Scouts from other races who had ventured into their territory had failed to return alive. The centaurs rarely ever communicated with any creature outside of their own, and when they did, it was usually by impaling them on the end of their long spears.

But if his father had decided he was angry with Myrddin, then he would sacrifice the fate of the entire kingdom if it meant keeping the message away from him. The thought made his blood boil, but he pushed his feelings aside. He could not imagine how the commander had managed to get the message to him. It must have taken quite some sleight of hand.

Evakhan and Bayard both stared intently as the prince untied the thin piece of twine which held the roll together and unraveled the message. Once opened, the parchment was still not very big, only about the size of his palms, which, although they were a fair bit larger than human palms, were not very large at all.

Myrddin's jaw dropped as he read the message.

"Well?" asked Evakhan, hopping expectantly from one foot to the other. "What does it say?"

Bayard placed his hand on the young elf's shoulder and gave him a stern look. Evakhan collected himself and stood patiently, or at least as patiently as he could, while the prince stared at the message.

"The centaurs," the prince started, unsure of how to voice exactly what they had said to him, "have recognized me as one of their own."

"What?" Bayard and Evakhan both exclaimed in surprise.

The prince nodded his head in confirmation, realizing his face had betrayed his shock at the note's contents. He heard his father's voice in his head, scolding him for his lapse in royal decorum. Allowing underlings to observe one's true emotions was unseemly.

"The centaurs have seen me in their visions and they have given me counsel. They acknowledge my own ability to look into the future, just like their seers, and they say they regard me as a brother."

"What sort of counsel?" Evakhan asked, his brows drawn in concern.

The prince had often confided in his younger friend about the fact the way his abilities with dreams and visions, including the way they had made him feel isolated from the others, and seemed to provide his father with one more reason to reject him. The news of being embraced by such a violent and mercurial race as the centaurs seemed too good to be true, and as likely to be a trap as an offer of friendship.

"I'm afraid that I cannot tell you that, my friend," the prince said with a concerned smile. His expression showed that he was skeptical too, but his face turned from suspicion to wonder as he read the last line of the message that the centaurs had sent him.

'For the good of your race, and ours.'

Looking at Bayard, he said, "I'm going to have to leave the city before the end of the day I think."

Evakhan could not help his gaping mouth at the prince's comment, made worse yet by the fact that Bayard only nodded in understanding.

"The king does not wish to receive you at this moment," the older elf commented. "You might be gone for some time before he notices."

The prince looked at Bayard for a moment and then gave the older elf a slow nod with a grave expression. The commander had chosen a side, and it was not the current king's. Myrddin took a deep breath as the gravity of this moment sunk in. Then he drew himself up into an attitude of strength and confidence as he turned toward Evakhan.

"I know you are worried, but I need to go." He smiled warmly at his friend and placed his hand firmly on his shoulder. "I'm going to need someone to pick up on my duties so that I can be gone for even longer before the king is aware. He will likely punish you when he finds out though."

The king had forbidden that any of the elves set foot out of the castle walls, and Myrddin was the prince, his only heir that was risking his life by going on such a dangerous errand. Anyone caught aiding in such an act of rebellion would be treated severely.

"I'll do it," the young elf said with a nod. Myrddin's

"Thank you, my friend," Myrddin said, his eyes moistening as he gave his friend a nod of appreciation.. "I hope you will not have to do so for long."

Evakhan nodded in agreement. Then shivered the second Myrddin turned away to address Bayard.

"I'm going to need maps of the land, the most recent ones that we have, particularly of the lands to the south."

"I'll do what I can," the commander nodded. "Where shall I meet you with them?"

"Here, one hour."

Without another word, they all turned away. Evakhan going to complete the duties that he knew the prince had in the next few days, and to find out if there were any duties that he did not know of, Bayard to go and steal every political map that was currently being used to track the positions of the other races around the world, and Myrddin to sharpen his sword and pack as many supplies as possible into an unassuming bag.

The elf prince hoped that none of them would regret this day too much.

Myrddin slipped back to his rooms, again trying his best not to appear as if he was rushing. This manner of moving through the castle was becoming a habit. When he finally arrived, he dropped his facade of relaxation and rushed around the room as quickly as he could.

He found his small leather bag, only big enough to carry a skin of water, a fresh tunic only slightly thicker than the one that he was currently wearing, and his breakfast of a few stale pieces of bread that had been delivered to his room when he had not eaten with the other elves. He tried to place a dagger in the little bag as well, but it just would not fit without looking suspicious, so he slipped the knife into the back of his boot. The cold, hard touch of the steel against his foot gave him a strange sense of comfort. His sword, which he hastily sharpened before strapping to his waist, was impossible to hide.

He thought through a number of reasons and excused for carrying the sword, as well as any other challenges he might face if he encountered curiosity on his way out.

The sun was high in the sky by the time came to meet Bayard. He was glad that he would leave in broad daylight. Not only would it be somewhat less suspicious if someone saw him, but he would also be able to get as far away from the castle as possible before the light faded. He was rather excited at the opportunity to spend an afternoon in the sun after such a long time in the gloom of the castle.

He passed a few elves early on his journey to the outskirts of the castle. Being the prince, he couldn't help but be recognized, but he smiled genially and met their eyes with a gracious nod. This inevitably resulted in the other elves smiling and bowing their heads in deference. Hopefully, the passers-by would just remember his smile and regard for them, and not pay any attention to the direction he was going, or what he was carrying.

The further away from the depths of the caste he got, the fewer others he encountered, until finally he was walking alone. He entered the corridor just as Bayard did. The dark-haired elf rushed towards the prince, a piece of paper folded over many times in his hands.

"This is the best that I could do for you on such short notice, the rest are all locked up in the libraries and the others would be able to tell if I took them," the man said, showing to the pieces of paper as he passed them into the hands of the prince. "They are about a hundred years old, but I don't think the world has changed all that much. Maybe a few new trees and a river or two where it shouldn't be."

"Thank you," the prince said, meeting the commander's eyes as he shook his hand. "I won't forget this."

The commander nodded.

"Just be safe, my prince," the man said. "The world is a dangerous place at the moment, particularly the south."

They clasped each other's shoulders briefly, and then left in opposite directions.

Chapter 4

The prince hastened through the outermost winding corridors into the remains of the old town. He moved silently, drawing upon his years of training to become a master of the sword and dagger. Myrddin thought back on those times as he slipped through the remains of the town. He had taken the training seriously, but as a young elf in the days not long after the Great Change, he never expected to use such skills since the elves were already withdrawing deeper and deeper into the safety of the castle.

Myrddin kept close to the remains of the old homes, staying in the shadows as much as possible. He checked his feet carefully to make sure he did not step on any twigs, and juggled keeping his eyes forward, as well as observing the treetops above him. He had only been sent out to scout a few times before his father had deemed the role too dangerous for a prince of the elves, and because of his lack of experience, he had no clue where the scouts would be.

Perhaps it was fate, or merely luck, but he somehow managed to avoid them altogether. Although, he would think much later on, if a scout spotted him, the chances of the scout reporting on him would be minimal. Throughout the years, the small population had come to like their prince and future ruler a lot more than the current one, and they would not be likely to betray him to king Dalen.

He was surprised by how quickly the tree cover thickened when he exited the city. The city was luscious, yes, and had many trees elegantly woven into and around the homes and other buildings, but the forests surrounding the city were something else altogether. The scraggly limbs and branches clumped and twisted together like withered hands grasping and wrapping around anything they could find. Most of them were completely leafless, and those which still had a few leaves were yellow and sickly. The soil appeared to have been stripped of the nutrients they needed to flourish. Even the aroma was not that of a healthy forest. Instead of damp soil and bark, it smelt like mildew and old parchment.

This sight made him angrier yet with the council and his father. They were supposed to care for the forest. The elves were bound to the forest and the forest to them. Retreating into the castle and neglecting the sacred woods was not only cowardly, it was abandoning a solemn responsibility. No wonder the elves had been waning in their magical abilities and insight.

It was disgusting.

Once he decided he was far enough from the city, had not been followed, and had covered his tracks sufficiently, he pulled out the folded map Bayard had given him.

He tried to head directly south, but he knew that was not the right direction and he would now need to compensate for the distance he had already travelled in order to make sure he ended up in the right location.

The tangles of bare trees cast darkness around him, making it difficult to read the map, and he didn't want to attract undue attention by conjuring any type of light. He closed his eyes for a moment, then held the parchment at an angle barely catching a pale shaft of light which cut a slit through the gloom. Myrddin scanned the map back and forth across the shaft of light until he had memorized the way. Fortunately, Bayard had acquired a quality map for him. It might not have been the most detailed, and the most up-to-date map in the Elven libraries. The ink was still dark against the pale pages and the lines were crisp and un-smudged.

Trying his best to remember the classes in which he excelled as a child, he calculated how far he had travelled using the position of the sun and made sure he was travelling in the right direction.

He placed the maps back into his bag and started travelling again.

Happy with the distance he had put between himself and the kingdom of the elves and knowing if his father sent out a search party it would probably likely not be for a couple of weeks, he became less careful about the trail he was leaving behind him. Focusing instead on the speed he was travelling, trying to maximize it wherever possible.

His long, Elven legs and powerful lungs allowed him to travel far faster than a human, and by the time the sun was starting to touch the horizon, the surrounding trees were thinning out, and he smelled the air becoming dry.

Satisfied with the distance he had covered on his first day, and not eager to travel in the dark in such unfamiliar territory, he made camp for the night.

He had packed nothing to make himself comfortable, having been too short on space, but he made do with what he had. He made use of the tree cover around him, in order to get himself off the ground, and away from at least some of the dangers the forest might hold.

Picking what appeared to be a tree with adequate root depth and as little rot as possible, he climbed a few feet up, until he was well above the head height of most creatures, including other elves. The twisting branches, while not attractive, created several nooks and crevices, some spacious enough for Myrddin to nestle himself into. He tucked himself into one of the thicker knots of branches and closed his eyes.

Despite his early morning and his long day of strenuous travel, he got little sleep. His mind raced with thoughts of meeting the centaurs, of the condition of his kingdom and his forest, and of what his father's reaction would be once he realized what Myrddin had done. Dawn broke to find him more tired than before.

According to the centaurs, he had until late afternoon to get to their chosen meeting place. He estimated he was slightly ahead of schedule, but he was not sure of what the terrain ahead would look like, and so he was unwilling to waste time. As soon as he had enough light to see a few meters in front of him, he set off again.

His legs were numb and stiff at the start, and he struggled to maintain the speeds he maintained the day before, but he quickly got the blood flowing through them again, and he travelled faster yet, motivated by the thought of finally being of some use to the Elven people who depended on him, and trusted in him.

The tree cover continued to thin, and the ground flattened as he travelled. The darkness of the twisted woods was replaced with bright sun and blue skies with white clouds. At least the sky had not been blighted by all of the hardship and chaos. That notion, combined with the anticipation of the momentous meeting boosted his spirit. With less than an hour to spare, he reached his destination.

Myrddin pulled out his map and the note from the centaurs to double check his location. Yes, this was the designated spot, without doubt. He looked around with an expression of mild confusion and disappointment.

There was nobody to greet him, and nothing nearby to indicate a meeting place whatsoever.

Instead, he stood alone in an empty field, surrounded by low hills on all sides. The only sound was the wind softly rustling through the long blades of grass which rose all the way to his hips.

He contemplated a variety of scenarios. Perhaps the map he had been given by Bayard had a place name which had changed in the last few years. Perhaps another place had a name which was the same or similar. But none of those options made sense. This was definitely the "Oat fields of Chilgar". He had reached his destination.

He looked around more closely, wondering if the centaurs might have left a hidden clue or message for him somewhere nearby. The centaurs were wary and odd in their ways, so perhaps there was a test or riddle or some sort which he needed to solve before they showed themselves. If was the case, he'd failed, because he couldn't find anything of the sort.

As he looked around in frustration, he couldn't help also looking up and seeing once more just how lovely the sun and the sky were. The warmth and of the sun and the lushness of the tall grass eased the prince's mood. Perhaps he was simply too early. He decided to make himself comfortable, lying down amidst the long grass, watching the bright blue sky he so rarely got to enjoy.

This reverie gave him a few moments of priceless peace. He was an elf prince in a sunny pasture, far removed from the strife and chaos of his people, his world, and his family. He closed his eyes and drank in the warmth on his face and the earthy scent of oat grass.

He was drifting off into a desperately needed sleep when he noticed something unusual.

The ground was vibrating beneath him.

Not a constant vibration, but rather a rhythmic thump. It was almost as if some grand army was marching towards him. No, two armies coming toward him from both directions.

He vaulted to his feet. His head jerked around, trying to find the source of the surrounding noise, but he saw nothing. The field was empty. The only disturbance was the slight movement of the grass produced by the rhythmic thumping, which was still barely noticeable.

Realizing his eyes were not sufficient, he used his next best option, his magic. He reached out slowly with it, focusing his mind and inner senses to stretch out from him.

It slowly left his body in tendrils, like an octopus, allowing him to sense his surroundings in a way which transcended physical sight or touch. He experienced the living energy. He connected his life to the life within the grass, and the great and small creatures in the hills all around him.

They mostly appeared as a dull, glowing green in his mind. Different shades and levels of brightness showing the vitality of the plants, animals, and soil. He stretched further over the nearby hills until he touched something so cold and dark it felt like a pit of death among all the life or the hills and plains. It was a horrifying blackness, a nothingness, not merely the absence of magic, but almost an opposite, life-sucking energy.

He had found the machine army.

Interspersed between the army of robots and drones he sensed creatures of different intensities of magic, glowing like lanterns in the night. Dwarves, humans, MoleKind, a couple of different sprites and dryads, even a centaur or two. Then his mind was overwhelmed with a magical presence so powerful it shocked him out of his inner sight and back into the physical world.

Dragons.

As he pulled together the images from his mind with the growing sounds and vibrations, he could tell the battle was near. Likely just over the nearby hills and rolling in his direction.

He shook himself off and ran toward the hills to his left, in the army's direction, racing up the hills so quickly he did not notice the sheer cliff on the other side until he had already leapt from it. Fortunately, his Elven bones were strong, and he broke nothing as he landed harshly on the other side, although intense pain shot through his legs as he rolled, the skin being stripped from his body by the sandy earth beneath him.

He righted himself and stood in awe at the sight before him.

In his dreams, he had seen the army from the center, but now, from the outside, he truly marveled at the numbers. The drones and robots went on for as far as the eye could see. It was almost like staring into an ocean made of glinting metal, trying to make out the land on the other side, and being horribly unsuccessful.

An enormous shadow passed over him, drawing his eyes upward to a sight he had never thought he would lay his eyes on in his lifetime. A full-grown dragon in flight.

It was said that before the Great Change, the size of most dragons had been a bit larger than a horse, and while they mostly kept to themselves, there had been a number of encounters between dragons and other races which were quite friendly. Such encounters would often become the basis of bard's songs or tales told around campfires.

But even the dragons had been affected by the Great Change. One of their young died, and they became angry and isolated. Their rage and loss of connection to the other races fed upon itself so they grew and grew and grew. Their legendary velvety skin had become coarse and barbed.

The dragon above him was the size of a mountain, with thorns and spikes of all kinds sticking out of it in all directions, even on the ends of its wings. Its eyes were fierce and the wind from his wings made it hard for the prince to stand.

A deafening roar erupted from the dragon's mouth, and with it came a river of fire. Several attacking drones melted instantly, raining liquid metal onto the ground below. Others were damaged, spinning out of control in all directions with a sickening whine, sputtering and crashing into nearby trees. But others yet dodged the dragon's blast, like an ocean being parted, before they returned to their original positions and fired at the dragon.

Some of the rapidly moving projectiles and beams of intense heat simply bounced off the massive beast, but occasionally something would find its way through, and the heavens rained red, the sacred blood of the magical creature spilling onto those fighting beneath it.

The prince was not sure why the machines were marching, or where they were marching to, but he knew he was not willing to watch the living creatures get slaughtered. Without another thought, his sword was in one hand, his long dagger in the other, and he lunged at the metal beast closest to him.

His weapons merely glanced off the machine, and the creature continued to move forward as if nothing had happened. Not only was this disappointing, but the prince suddenly found himself sucked into the battle. The rapid movement of the robot forces pushed and shoved him, unyielding metal against his pliable body. Before he knew it he was completely surrounded by the battle.

All around him, he saw different races, a few elves like himself, dwarves, centaurs, dryads, and others. There were fewer of them than there were of the robots, and their numbers were dropping quickly. Even with the help of the dragons, which was rare these days, they would not win the battle.

Nevertheless, he continued to fight, swinging his sword in every direction, hoping to inflict what damage he could. A dwarf drew up alongside him, the sturdy creature's bright red hair and beard catching his attention. He swung a massive hammer around in circles, sometimes glancing off the machines, other times managing to find a spot weak enough to make a dent, or occasionally a crushing blow.

It was the appearance of the dwarf that shocked him into the realization that he was now experiencing the fulfillment of his vision. Every detail was the same, including the most terrifying detail of all.

He was going to die.

The robot with the spinning blades approached as before.

Time slowed to a standstill. Prince Myrddin of the Elves thought about the dream and how it had played out as he had foreseen. Or was his mind simply playing tricks on him in his last moments? Had there ever been a dream, or was he perhaps dreaming now?

Myrddin thought about his father and how news of the prince's failure would confirm his low opinion of his son. He thought about his sister and took comfort in the fact that in a few seconds, he would be united with her in the Second Life. He took a deep breath and was about to close his eyes to meet his fate when something unexpected happened.

A nearby robot, one which he had paid little attention to as it wasn't attacking him, turned toward the robot in front of him. This strange new robot swept a blade which protruded from its hand behind of the blades of the other robot, slicing the bladed arms from the prince's attacker. The movement happened so quickly the prince could feel the air moving as the blades rushed past his face.

Its arms fell harmlessly, plowing furrows into the ground before coming to a halt. The new robot touched the side of the attacker with its other "hand" which emitted blue sparks, a crackling noise, and the smell of lightning during a thunderstorm. The attacking robot shuddered and sputtered, falling backwards into a convulsing heap.

Barely able to move, but wary of this new robot, Myrddin stood to defend himself. He gathered just enough strength to raise his blade in front of him. But instead of attacking him, this new robot moved perpendicularly to the movement of the rest of the robots, attacking more of its own.

Although Myrddin was confused, he understood this robot appeared to be protecting him. He mused at the very idea, and was sure his father, full of hatred, would shout at him at that moment, chastising him for being an idiot. But he was not his father, and something deep within him told him this creature, whatever it was, was trustworthy.

He watched another robot opening the compartment in its shoulders which contained the lethal, rapidly shooting projectiles the humans had referred to as 'bullets' in the time before the change. It was pointed at the new robot, the different one. This strange creature was now the one in danger.

In the few moments since he had seen it, it had not once used one of these weapons itself, even though such a projectile weapon would have logical choice for combat, so he assumed this new robot must not have been equipped with such a weapon.

His body rushed forward, almost of its own accord, and his sword stretched out in front of the robot, deflecting the bullet before it connected with this allied robot's head. The thing spared him only a small glance, seeming to nod its head slightly before it continued its battle.

They fought together in such a way for a long time, felling or avoiding the machine soldiers and protecting each other. The sun had turned the sky purple, and the prince could see only red on the ground, from the blood of the dragons, and the blood of the other creatures which had perished during the battle.

Had the ground not been so dry, eagerly sucking up every bit of moisture it could get from the surface, Myrddin was sure they would have been slipping and sliding in the stuff.

Then, almost as quickly as the battle had started, it was over. The end of the robot army had passed them. They were out on the other side and the machine army marched away, ignoring them and the destruction they had left in their wake.

For quite some time, they could still hear the steady thunder of the machine army marching steadily in the other direction, but the few creatures which were still alive did not have the strength to pursue and fight them. Instead, they all stood around blankly, or sank to the ground, grateful to have survived.

The prince's body felt numb, his throbbing wound was the only reassurance he had that he was still alive.

Looking around, a knot formed in his throat. The warriors who had battled the army had not been many to start, but now there were less than ten remaining. The plain was littered with the corpses of their fallen comrades.

There were machines too, crushed and cut apart. But the number seemed pathetic compared to the hordes which had marched past them. This was not a victory. This was a slaughter, and it was unclear to the prince if, from the robots' perspective if this had even been a battle, or a minor nuisance on their way to... wherever they were going.

In the distance, the prince saw one of the remaining living creatures, one of the few centaurs who had fought. This itself was a great surprise. The centaurs seldom involved themselves with other races, much less to lend support. For them to have lifted a finger in this battle, so far from their own home, the centaurs must have considered this battle worthy of their own risk and sacrifice. That, combined with the participation of the mighty dragons, filled him with a sense of wonder, and of dread.

The centaur saw the prince gazing at it, and nodded its head at him, raising its spear above its head in salute, before turning from the field and galloping away with a fearsome battle cry.

As the sound faded, so did the prince's vision, blurry blackness creeping in from the corners. With what little he had left of his sight, he gazed down at his torso. It was completely shredded and soaked in blood. He was surprised he had survived as long as he had.

And with that thought, he sank to his knees, and the darkness overtook him.

Chapter 5

Myrddin awoke slowly and painfully. His body ached and his mind was hazy. He tried unsuccessfully to shake off the fog. He tried to scan the room quietly, without moving his body.

What he saw was so bizarre and other-worldly he thought he was still dreaming. It appeared he had been swallowed up by one of the robots. The idea made him dizzy. He dropped his head back on the pillow and closed his eyes.

He dozed again, and the sun was well above the mountains when he finally got up from his resting place. He was definitely awake now, but his surroundings were every bit as surreal, and they had been a few hours ago.

All around him were metallic components, robot parts. In some places, the brightly colored wires from inside the machines hung from the walls and the roofing. He recognized other parts from the robots he had fought in the fields. Arms, chest plates, blades, gun barrels, and scrap metal surrounded him. Most were strewn about randomly, but some, especially the weapon parts, appeared to be organized by size and category.

With consciousness and a clear mind also came awareness of the sharp pain in his side. He realized he was not in the belly of a robot or drone, but in a cave which had been made from the scrap of machine parts. A graveyard for the unnatural beings. He was surrounded by robot bodies.

This macabre image reverberated in the elf's mind, developing into a panic. The prince was fearless in battle and not afraid of death or what awaited after. But being stuck in the graves of creatures which were never alive in the first place struck a sickening chord in his spirit. He fought past the pain and stiffness and tried to rise, looking for an exit from this horrific place.

As he did, he heard a scraping sound, accompanied by the thunk of metal on metal. Someone, or rather something, was coming.

He looked around the room, searching desperately for a place to hide, but no space was large enough to conceal his body. So he did the only thing he could think of. He laid back down and pretended he had never regained consciousness.

After a little more scuffling, he was surprised to see, through his slotted eyes, opened just enough for him to make out the vaguest outlines of the surrounding space, that a panel in the wall slid open to reveal a door where previously there had been none. He tried to breathe as evenly as possible, despite his racing heart, as he waited for whatever it was to come into the room.

To his surprise, the being entering the room was the same creature which had fought beside him. Robot-looking for sure, yet not like any he had seen before. But now he could see a little better, it appeared to be made up of scraps of different machines he had seen on the battlefield. An odd conglomeration of other creatures into a new one. It had a humanoid, shape like most other robots, but slightly wider and shorter. Its motion seemed off as well, somehow out of kilter with way the other robots moved.

It was disgusting.

He could not imagine having to make use of Evakhan's arm, or Bayard's foot if something were to happen to his own. The whole idea was vulgar, unnatural. The knots of fear in his stomach turned to nausea at the thought.

The creature turned to him, forcing him to slam his eyes shut again. He had allowed them to creep further and further open to try to catch a better view of the thing without realizing. He focused on his breathing as he strained his ears, not daring to open his eyes as much as a sliver to see what the creature was doing.

He heard its quiet, measured steps as it came close to him. To his surprise, the creature was deliberately trying to be quiet, completely unlike the machines he had seen out on the battlefield. Those creatures, grinding and whirring and stamping their heavy feet on the ground, were oblivious to the racket they created.

Eventually, the monstrosity stood right beside him. He struggled to keep his breath slow and steady. He strained his ears, trying to discern exactly how close this monster was to him, trying to determine if he might need to jump up and try to escape if the beast tried to dissect him, or something equally horrific. As he listened, the creature's own breath gave its position away.

it was looming right over his face.

The realization came over him with a jolt. His eyes involuntarily started to open, but he stopped them in time. Because he realized something else.

The creature staring down at him was breathing. And machines did not breathe. This was not a machine at all.

After a minute of observation, it seemed to be satisfied with its analysis of him and stepped away, walking to the opposite wall of the little room. Once it was far enough away from him, he eased his eyes open again.

He watched as the creature, bent over to remove what Myrddin had originally thought were its feet, but he now realized were boots, fashioned out of the outermost steel plates of the walking robots.

The thing unsnapped a lever on the side of its neck, then twisted its upper area sideways as if to remove its own head. The prince was about to gasp out loud as the helmet released, allowing the creature to remove the head covering, revealing the long, dark hair of a woman. A human woman.

"What... are... you?" His voice was hoarse from the lack of use, and the words barely escaped his mouth. But in the otherwise silent environment, they echoed like a battle gong.

In the days following, it would occur to the prince that this was probably not the most gracious way to greet someone whom he had fought alongside and who had obviously saved his life. But he was doing the best he could just then.

The woman jumped. She had been removing her steel gloves and had obviously not been expecting anyone to speak.

She spun around and they studied each other carefully, each with an oddly similar mixture of suspicion and wonder in their eyes. She had high cheekbones, almost Elven in nature. Her hair was a deep brown and hung below her shoulders. Her eyes were the bluish gray of the sea before a storm, currently pulled into a wary frown.

"I am a human," she whispered matter-of-factly, her eyes still searching his. He saw her holding something behind her back, which she had grabbed before he could see what it was. But he was wise enough to gather it was probably a weapon.

He nodded slightly, although a thoughtful expression appeared on his face. She was obviously a human, but he was having trouble believing it. "But I thought humanity had all died out a long time ago, and the only remnants were the..."

He stopped, so she completed his sentence for him.

"The MoleKind. Yes, I know," she spat out in disgust. Her demeanor changed instantly to disgust with what sounded to the prince like a strong overreaction to the word.

"Those of us who are left don't like to show ourselves to the rest of the world," she continued. "Not that I have ever actually spoken to anyone much, but I am aware they exist," she shrugged, glaring at him as if to dare him to say something.

Her disguise, isolation, and her disgust toward the MoleKind started to make sense to the prince.

While all races had become isolated and suspicious of each other since the Great Change, humanity was the most despised race of all. The entire planet viewed them as the primary cause of the strife and decay which now plagued the once lovely world of Alyrraesia. If any of the other races were to meet an actual human, violence was likely. Most believed they had all been killed off long ago, and none mourned their passing.

He decided he would take advantage of this rare opportunity to speak to such a creature and learn more about them. The Elven libraries were vast, but they were not infinite, nor were they conclusive, especially regarding humans.

"Where did you come from?" he asked, as politely as possible, deciding to start with a simple question to figure out what would and would not be acceptable to the human, or so he thought.

"From two human parents, just like you probably came from two elf parents," she quipped sarcastically, the annoyance clear in her voice.

His frustration grew, but he kept it in check. Shaking his head and speaking more softly, he tried again.

"Why did you help me if you knew I was an elf?" The humans and the elves had never been close allies. Since the Great Change the animosity had turned to open hatred in both directions.

"Because you were fighting against those robots," the human said flippantly. He noticed her hand had yet to leave the weapon behind her back and she had yet to step any closer to him.

"Nobody has seen an elf for quite a long time either. They say they have hidden themselves away, deep in their old cities, and they will only reemerge when this war is finished, one way or the other."

She emphasized the last few words to drive home her point, then took one step closer. "Yet here you are." She pointed at him with both arms, revealing the rusty blade she had been concealing, and waving it at him menacingly.

He grimaced at the implications of her words. The elves, born to be a gracious and social race, the center of trade and enchantment, now had earned a reputation as cowardly recluses.

"Here I am, I suppose," he said absentmindedly, ignoring knife which was brandished in his direction.

The human reacted to his lackluster answer with a quizzical stare.

"You are regretting leaving?" she asked, taking a step closer, holding her blade up the entire time.

He took a long pause before speaking, as he wasn't completely sure himself of the answer. "No. I thought for a moment I might, a day or so after I left," he said, thinking back to the pain he would cause Evakhan and Bayard when his absence, and their complicity in it was discovered, "but the longer I stay out here the more I find myself happy I did."

Bayard and Evakhan were loyal servants and soldiers. If they would be happy to endure political and reputational difficulty for a little while, then that was a sacrifice he was willing to make. Or rather, a sacrifice he was willing to allow them to make.

The human nodded, then winced as she at the side of his abdomen, still bloody and shredded. He was sure he looked as if he was on his deathbed to a human, who would not have survived such injuries for more than a few minutes.

Her gaze softened, and she slowly lowered her weapon, taking one step closer.

"I'm not sure if you are going to live," she whispered. The suspicion in her eyes melted into compassion, almost pity. This was the first time he had seen her display an emotion other than anger or disgust. Carrying this expression, her face was rather lovely.

In his guarded state, he pushed back the smile began to form. Then, upon further consideration, he allowed himself the indulgence and his lips broadened.

At least someone else still retained a measure of empathy for the other races. He was glad he was not alone in this but was surprised he had found a like-minded individual in a human of all things.

"I'll live," he reassured her, his smile widening.

For the first time since his injury, he examined his own wounds, studying them with his eyes and reaching within his mind to examine his inner self and how the damage was connected to him. He closed his eyes, took a deep breath, and held his hands up to his abdomen, hovering them as close to the wounds as possible without actually touching them, and started chanting.

The human's eyes widened as his hands started glowing. She instantly stepped away, raising her sword up in front of herself again. Myrddin didn't notice her, as his consciousness was focused fully on his task, his mind and body becoming one with the magic as his flesh knitted itself back to its intended condition.

Her weapon involuntarily dropped and she gazed curiously as the process continued. Exposed muscle slowly and deliberately restoring itself. It was like watching the injury happen in reverse. Blood stopped oozing from lacerations and began to flow through newly reformed vessels. Finally, a layer of fresh skin appeared, like butter somehow un-melting over the sinews. The wound in the front of his body was healed completely, but the one on his side remained as he took a deep sigh and opened his eyes.

"Magic?" she asked quietly once he had finished.

"Yes, a healing kind," he smiled as the wound tingled, numbed by the effects of the magic. If he had the proper herbs on him, he could have healed his side as well, and wouldn't be feeling the effects of the spell at all. As it was, the wounds stung, and his head swooned as his mind and body adjusted to its newly formed parts.

"That is amazing," she exclaimed, a little too loudly for his liking, rushing forward to examine his wound with clumsy fingers and causing of pain to shoot through his side again. He pulled away from her and she stopped short, her expression of wonder shifting back to its previous, guarded gaze.

Losing the warmth between them and remembering the loss of the dignity and culture of his people shocked Myrddin into an awareness of how brutish he had been with her so far. His lack of grace, his short, direct questions were not the etiquette of the Elven court. When did knowing a creature's race become more important than knowing their name? It was no wonder the elves had lost their reputation and so far; he had done nothing to gain it back.

"I have not yet thanked you for bringing me to this place of safety. Please accept my deepest gratitude." He began, watching for her expression to soften before he continued. "May I ask your name?"

"Oh, sorry," she replied, looking a little sheepish. "I suppose in all the excitement I forgot to tell you. I'm called Ava."

"Ava?" he tested the name on his tongue. It differed from names the elves gave, yet it had a pleasant sound. Clear, symmetrical, elegant in its own way. "That's a lovely name. Very human-sounding, but strong and... lovely." He winced at his inability to come up with a different word, but she didn't seem to mind.

"Thank you. I'm glad you approve." Having never spoken to a human before and being unfamiliar with their culture and manner of speaking, he was unsure if her reply was genuine, sarcastic, or something in between. He thought he might have been imagining in the dim light, but he thought her cheeks tinged pink. She ducked her head and replied, "I am told it was my mother's name."

Ah, apparently she had taken his statement as a compliment, and the sarcasm was a form of warm joking. Myrddin continued.

"Where are we?" he asked, gesturing with his hands at the room and its contents.

She was about to answer him when a grating sound echoed through the little room from the outside.

Ava's demeanor snapped from the calm pose she had slowly fallen into, to standing bolt upright, the rusty blade held so tightly in her grubby hand her knuckles turned white. He imagined if she had hair like a cat, it would be standing on end.

His eyes met hers. Slowly, a single finger moved in front of her lips. Apparently, the sign for "be quiet" was universal.

They waited for some time. The sound continued, growing louder and louder, before diminishing again. Myrddin recognized the rhythmic steps of several robots combined with the sliding of metal on metal. He froze, bracing himself in case he needed to run or fight.

Eventually, the sounds died out and he dared to whisper to the human, "Is it safe now?"

She paused before answering, her face scrunched up as she focused, trying to make out the sound of the robots. But she heard nothing. Not even Myrddin's Elven ears registered anything.

"For the time being," she said, still whispering.

"Where are we?" he asked, gesturing to the room in which they stood. The robot parts, combined with the presence of the robots outside, did not make for an ideal living space, yet the human had clearly been living here for quite some time. She appeared quite accustomed to the activities and her responses were refined in a practiced manner.

"We are in one of the old robot scrap yards. They discard anything here that's faster for them to remake than it is for them to repair or melt down," she sounded frustrated with having to explain the situation to him, almost as if she expected him to know it already.

"And the sound... was them?"

"Yes, it was," she said, again looking mildly annoyed, as if replying to a child. "But not the battle machines you saw before. What you heard is the sound of non-military robots, large, slow, hulking things. They scavenge the battlefields and drop their scraps into heaps like the one surrounding this bunker."

It made sense. He knew sometimes it was easier for the machines to discard damaged parts and simply replace them with newly made ones. It required less energy than converting the older parts. But this was not a place for any normal creature to dwell in temporarily. He would avoid this place by any means if he was simply travelling through this area, and would not even consider trying to live here.

"How long have we been here?" he asked, grimacing as he shifted, both due to the pain in his side and the idea of being so close to the creatures at all times.

"Well, you've been out for a couple of hours," Ava said, eyeing the side of his once-fine tunic, which was lacerated and covered in dried blood.

"And you?"

She paused for a moment, seeming to contemplate how to best answer his question. Resolve strengthened in her eyes before she spoke up. "For a long time."

He nodded, understanding this would fall into the category of sensitive topics he would have to be careful about. Her voice was harsh and her tone was final. He dropped the subject for the time being.

Instead, he pointed to the armor she was still wearing. As he looked closer, he realized she had fashioned the torso, gauntlets, leggings, and assorted weapons in a rather clever and skillful way. A dwarf of the old days might actually have been impressed with her ingenuity in metalwork.

"The armor you wear," he said, "it makes you look like a robot."

She rolled her eyes, more condescending than ever, as she looked down at herself, "Which is kind of the point. The parts are readily available here. It's the easiest and strongest thing for me to have to protect myself, and if I look like one of them then they..." She paused, her eyes darkening into a sad frown. "And... most other creatures... tend to leave me alone."

He paused in surprise before he continued. "You want to be left alone?" he asked softly.

"That's not what I said." She snapped. "It's just healthier than being a human in the midst of all the other races."

The elf prince bowed his head. No doubt she had suffered at the prejudice of other races, including his own. Humans were certainly a despised race, but he was shocked she considered herself safer disguised as a robot than to be seen in her true form.

As Myrddin considered this, he thought about his father and his own sense of being considered a failure and a castaway.

"I understand". He stated calmly.

"I doubt you do," her laugh was dry, "but thanks for pretending."

He simply shook his head.

"What are your reasons for being out of the mighty Elven fortress anyway?" She asked in a much more gentle and conciliatory tone than before.

He considered his answer before speaking. If she understood the current reputation of the elves, she would be aware of their harsh king who was driving their culture of isolation and selfishness. Myrddin was not anxious to be recognized as the son and heir of this legacy.

"I saw a vision." he started slowly, "I vision of the future which which has since come to pass. And after seeing the vision I received a message from a centaur telling me to meet them."

"A centaur!" she exclaimed. "I thought I saw one looking at you strangely on the battlefield. I've never seen one of them pay attention to anyone or anything else, other than trying to kill it."

He nodded in agreement, "They are a peculiar race, which is why I paid such careful attention to the message, and the vision."

"I thought only centaurs had those kinds of visions," she said, confused, "Like it was something to do with magic itself."

"I thought so too, but so many other things have changed. Magic itself seems to be shifting, reorganizing itself I suppose." He replied.

"Do you think you will have another?" She asked, her eyes widening with wonder.

He met her expression with a dark and painful gaze before lowering his head.

"I don't know. I truly hope not," he said. "If you humans understood the burden and the responsibility which comes with magic..."

He felt himself about to scold her for something which wasn't her fault and stopped himself. They sat without speaking for a long moment. Only the hum of the dim yellow lights above them interrupted the silence.

"What are you going to do next?" She eventually asked.

"Honestly, I do not know," he replied. He leaned back thoughtfully against the cushion Ava had crafted from padding and packing materials.

"My latest vision was of the battle we experienced." He mused out loud. "It was confirmed down to the last detail. The machines have built an organized army and are on an offensive march to some unknown goal. All the other races seem to be fighting them, but without communication or coordination." He gave a dry and disgusted laugh. "Well, all the races except one. If I were to go back and tell my people, they would simply retreat even further into their hole."

She stared at him for a moment, and appeared to want to say something, but changed her mind, shaking her head. This happened a few times before she eventually put a sentence together which she seemed to be satisfied with.

"If I knew where they were going, would that help in your decision?" she asked quietly.

"Perhaps," he said slowly, lifting his head with interest.

She struggled with the decision to reply, but then blurted out her statement so quickly he had to pause a moment to make sense of the words that had come tumbling out of her mouth.

"They head to a place called Last Chance." she said.

The prince sat up. "Last Chance?" He responded, the name and its implication sinking in. "This place is not known among the elves. Is it some sort of refugee camp?"

"Yes," Ava confirmed, "nobody goes there unless they have nowhere else to go. For many people, it is their 'Last Chance' of survival, hence the name."

"And how do you know of this place?" he asked curiously.

She shrugged her shoulders. "A lot of the people I come across, or rather observe, are on their way there. People don't come through these parts unless they are desperate, and Last Chance is usually where the desperate ones are going."

He noted she said she only observed the people coming through these parts, and not interacting with them. He thought of the poor, terrified souls, so desperate they were willing to make their way through a junkyard of robots to get to where they were going.

"Do you think it really is the people's Last Chance?" he asked.

She shrugged yet again. She seemed to do that a lot. "Don't know. Not my problem."

"And the robot army is heading there?" he asked.

"I don't know if that's their target or not, but the direction they're headed, they can't miss it," she stated flatly.

Myrddin tried to jump up, but the pain halted him. Ava moved to help him up, but he waved her off. After taking a breath, he exclaimed. "We need to warn those people, they need to at least know what is coming for them."

Ava took a step back from him and crossed her arms, which still bore her metal gauntlets, looking down at him and speaking angrily. "You think you can get there on time in your condition?" she asked. "And what do you mean, 'We?'"

"We don't have any other option, do we?" he replied, his anger rising to meet hers. "If we don't warn them of what is coming, they will be massacred. If we warn them, maybe some of them could evacuate in time."

The human looked him up and down, probably assessing the state he was in, before turning away. He could not miss the look of pity and frustration on her face.

"Those people are not my responsibility! I've never even spoken to them, because if I tried to, half of them would have simply killed me on sight. And you. You'll never get there by yourself on foot, not even if you were perfectly healthy. And look at the state you are in. "

They locked stared for a long moment. Then Myrddin broke the silence with a frustrated sigh.

"Very well. You have made your decision. I will neither force nor beg you to accompany me." He rose slowly, testing his legs and walking around the room as he continued. "But for me, I am sickened to death to live in a world where nobody cares for anyone but themselves. Where races who used to live in harmony and cooperation now only meet on the battlefield, and my own people don't even do that.

Even the centaurs and the dragons stand and fight while my own..." He stopped himself, took a breath, and concluded.

"If I succeed, I will have spared lives. If I fail, then perhaps word will spread that one of those cowardly, selfish elves risked himself to protect others."

Ava continued to stare at him and shook her head, arms still crossed. Then, with a sigh, she grabbed her helmet and the various other items of her armor she had removed when she had first entered. She also grabbed a few small items, gesturing to his bag, which was still in surprisingly good condition.

He passed it to her reluctantly and was surprised when she started pushing little bits of what looked like cured and dried fruits and meats into it. She even refilled his water skin after finding it.

"If you are so adamant, then I think I may know a way you can get there quicker," she said as she rushed around, opening up compartments in the walls which he had not realized were there before retrieving the relevant items.

"You do?" he asked in surprise, shocked at her sudden change in demeanor.

She nodded her head. "The machines will have to cross a mountainous ridge to get there. I know of an underground tunnel which will take you through the mountain instead. You might use it to your advantage and gain a little time while they have to deal with the extra distance. It will still be close though."

He paused for a moment, noting her use of pronouns, "you", not "we". She would not accompany him. She was probably only helping him in order to get him out of her home. He didn't speak, but simply bowed his head in thanks before making his way toward where he knew the panel would slide open to reveal the door. He made sure his sword was firmly fastened at his waist, and his dagger was securely in his boot.

"You need to leave as quickly as possible," she said, as she waited for him to get close enough to the panel in the wall, her hand on a lever he could not see, which he assumed would open the panel. But she paused, a troubled look crossing over her face.

"What's wrong?" he asked.

She hesitated again, unsure. "What is your name, elf? I have told you mine, but I don't know yours."

He could not help the small chuckle which escaped him. He could see how she would have felt some discomfort. They had been talking for quite some time, and he knew her name. It would normally be socially unacceptable to ask for someone's name this late, in all polite races and cultures. But this was no ordinary situation, to be sure, and the only thing less polite at this point would have been to withhold it.

"I am called Myrddin," he said with a short bow.

She thought for a moment before trying it out. It sounded odd on her tongue; her mouth not used to making the sounds required for Elven names. She did not quite get the correct undertones which would have come naturally to even a child. But he did not mind.

"Myrddin. That is a very Elven name," she commented wryly.

He smiled at her irritation. If only she knew. It was a name reserved specifically for use by the royal Elven family. There were few names which were quite as purely Elven. "It is," he confirmed.

She opened the panel without another word, placing her foot on the small of his back and shoving him out quickly. "Well, Myrddin, it's time for you to leave."

Chapter 6

T he moment the panel slid open in front of him, he had to resist the urge to gasp in shock. Rubbing his eyes with disbelief, combined with the kick from the human, he almost fell forward onto his face.

As far as the eye could see there was only steel. The ground below their feet, steel. The small hills surrounding them, steel. The only color present was the insulation of the abandoned electrical components. Even the sky was a dull grey, like steel.

His body was jerked back as a drone whisked around the corner of one of the many piles, carrying some components itself. He caught a glimpse from around the corner to observe the buzzing menace fly all the way to the top of a pile before releasing the components. They clanged and clattered as they tumbled down the pile, and a few other pieces were hoisted loose, sending a component avalanche down the side of the pile. The drone flew away without looking back.

"Over here." Ava said whispered, pointing to a pile of discarded robot parts which resembled all the other piles of discarded robot parts. "About a league or two. We've made sure there are a couple of old red parts, the paint's probably a bit flaky still, but it'll let you know you're in the right place."

"Thank you for your kindness," Myrddin started, but the human had already closed the panel which led to the opening of her home.

The prince was about to shout with indignation but thought better of it. He mused upon the woman's rudeness. Myrddin was the prince of his land, and although his father regularly treated him with disdain, he was accustomed to polite deference from everyone he encountered. He clearly wasn't home anymore.

Although, he genuinely wondered if the human's uncultured, brash behavior was due to a lack of social interaction, and more importantly, social education. Perhaps that was another luxury he had taken for granted all his life.

Shaking his head, he tried to calm his irritation with logical reasoning, without much success, and started moving. He was able to move quickly, although not nearly as fast as he would have liked. He struggled with the pain in his side and the resulting lack of mobility.

This, unfortunately, also meant he could'nt be as quiet as he would have liked to be otherwise.

His soft boots, with little stones stuck in the worn grooves of the soles, tapped and scratched against the metal below his feet; not only causing an alarming amount of noise but also sticking into his flesh. He smelled nothing but rust and dust in the air. All of this was foreign to him and, as a result, overwhelming.

Perhaps that was why he didn't notice the robots in the distance sooner.

When he spotted them, they were directly above him, on one of the tall heaps. The first indication of their presence was the tumbling of jostled parts down the steep escarpment. Next, he heard the hydraulic pumps in their joints as the wind was pushed out of them, allowing their stiff limbs to bend.

His head shot upwards, trying to find them, but they were hard to make out, surrounded by the body parts of their fallen comrades. Spotting them was like picking out a deer in a thick forest. The only thing which differentiated them from their surroundings was their movement.

They were older models, similar to the ones he had seen in the Elven libraries which had been created about twenty years before the change. They were humanoid, much like the other robots, but stockier. Instead of their bodies being designed for combat, with a tough and aerodynamic outer shell, with no rigid corners. They were made of a lightweight, flimsier material, and the segments of their bodies were slightly more cuboid.

The prince realized they were probably sent to this place to sort out the machine parts or to perform some other type of maintenance duties. They were clearly not designed for battle, but they were still formidable, and they could cause him quite a lot of harm in his damaged state. Plus, they might alert others if he did not dispatch them quickly.

The first robot reached the bottom just as he drew his enchanted sword. In the weak light, he could make out the dim glow, the ring of the steel as it left his scabbard echoing eerily through the place.

The robot lunged at him. It did not seem to have any compartments which might slide open to reveal a weapon, but its hands, which did not match his body, appeared to be a newer design. They had a collection of blades and spinning saws on the ends, similar to the spinning sawblades of the human's armor.

He dodged the initial attack and swung his sword at the blade arm, but to no avail. The reinforced steel of the newer design was too strong to cut and weapon merely glanced away. He struggled to raise his sword in time to defend from the second attack. This time he was fortunate enough to hook the edge of his blade in the teeth of some of the spinning saws, effectively grinding them to a halt.

This allowed him a moment to assess the situation better.

In the distance, he observed the second robot, who had not yet joined the battle. It had bent its body grotesquely until its legs, completely bent backwards, were placed on its back, anchoring the machine in place. The cavity in the front of its chest was busy sliding open slowly, creating a grating noise as rust slid against rust and old gears struggled to work.

From the cavity, the prince watched a massive cannon barrel extending, far larger than he had ever seen on any robot before. Judging by the way the machine anchored itself to the ground, the projectile about to be launched must be massive enough to have a strong recoil which would otherwise knock the robot over when launched. The torso of the monster slowly twisted, obviously working to aim the weapon at Myrddin.

He quickly pressed against his sword, trying to use what little momentum he had left after connecting with the machine in front of him, and he pushed it away, barely an inch. This gave him enough space to move his sword to strike at a weak spot which had been revealed under the creature's arm, where the joint meant the steel of the arm did not quite meet with the steel of the body.

His sword slid in with ease, releasing the compressed air within, paralyzing the arm.

He wriggled the blade around to destroy as many inner components as possible. This proved to be successful, as the bright red light which glowed in the eyes of all the robots slowly went dim. The machine's joints stiffened, and the robot crumpled to the ground.

He had no time to celebrate his success as the second robot had leveled its cannon's barrel right at the prince, making a whirring noise which grew higher in pitch and loudness.

Myrddin jumped to one side and rolled behind a disembodied robot torso to his left. From his position of cover, he watched a missile that was similar, but larger than the one which killed the dwarf, emerge from the barrel and fly toward the body of the robot he had been fighting. He flattened himself to the ground as the projectile struck the first robot and exploded, sending tiny shards of metal in all directions.

The older robot apparently couldn't adjust its aim once the missile had begun to launch. He'd remember that fact for the future. He rose as quickly as his injury would allow and ran for the remaining machine, but it had already reloaded and had turned to aim directly at him.

The whirring of the launch had already begun, and the prince didn't think he'd reach the robot before the missile fired. But momentum was already carrying him forward, and he hadn't recovered his dexterity enough to change direction quickly.

As he raised his sword and let out a final battle cry, a loud crunching and whirring sound rang through the air, and the robot started shuddering violently. The prince stared as the blur of a spinning sawblade emerged from the robot's neck. No, not from its neck, through its neck, causing the head to wobble from side to side as if the machine had become confused or drunk.

The body of the robot twisted upward and to the left, causing the rocket to miss the prince by several strides. The projectile flew for quite some distance before impacting and exploding, creating an enormous crater and an impressive shower of robot parts. The prince turned back to the robot as the remaining components in its neck were shredded by the spinning blade, and the severed head fell forward and rolled down the slope.

Behind the head was a sight he had not been expecting.

It was Ava, fully dressed in her robotic armor. She held a long, thick rod, with the spinning circular sawblades attached to the end. He observed the joints where she had welded the components of the weapon together, and where a few wires hung out, dangerously close to the blade. The design was homemade, but effective. He stared at her with an expression somewhere between relief and shock.

Before he could ask, she lifted her helmet, revealing her annoyed expression, and exclaimed, "You couldn't even last an hour without me?"

"You were following me?"

She replied sardonically. "Don't flatter yourself. I had already planned a scouting and scavenging trip in this direction. Now let's get out of here before all the noise you made brings the whole machine army down on us!"

They scurried across the piles of robot refuse to an alcove made from huge storage containers and the cover of an overhanging piece of steel from what used to be an automobile. The two of them sat in silence for several minutes, waiting to see if their encounter with the robots had attracted any attention.

"Seriously, why did you follow me?" he finally asked quietly.

She stared at him for a moment, saying nothing, before pointing to his side.

"You're injured, and I knew you wouldn't last long. I decided I couldn't have all the effort I put into keeping you alive for this long go to waste." She replied, a smug grin covering her face.

He rubbed his hands across his own face. "Now what?" he said, staring at her.

She studied him thoughtfully for a moment.

"Now... I'm going with you to Last Chance." Myrddin opened his mouth to reply, but she held up her robotic hand and continued matter-of-factly. "You're injured and you're not familiar with this terrain or how the robots work. I don't have any love or connection to any of the others, but you and I fought side by side, so I guess we're allies at least. I've got few enough of those, so I guess that's worth something."

"Thank you," he said.

"Don't thank me yet." She replied with a smile. "Look, I haven't had much company and I know I can be a little… "

She was about to continue when the whirring of a drone cut through the air just over their heads.

"We need to be careful out here," Ava whispered, putting her helmet back on her head, so quietly even his Elven ears didn't hear the sound. "You can hear some of them coming, but others you can't. We'll stick to the shadows."

He nodded and waved his hand for her to lead the way. He imagined his father would have scoffed at the idea of deferring to a human, but he regarded her as a fellow warrior, one who had specific and valuable information about the enemy and its tactics. She also knew exactly where they were going, which he did not.

They walked for some time, sticking close to the bottoms of piles, ducking under overhangs wherever possible. He was glad he had worn his leather boots. The soft, well-worn material made little noise on the metallic surface beneath them, whereas the human's steel boots struggled to allow them to move quietly.

They sprinted from cover to cover so quickly and rounded so many corners he was sure he would never be able to find his way back to the human's home if he needed to. Everything appeared the same, barren, and lifeless. It was not like the forest where each tree was unique and where he could sense the life and individuality in each of them. All the robots and their pieces looked the same to him and there was no sense of life or magic anywhere. The scene was disorienting and sickening to his elven senses.

He couldn't even discern which direction they were travelling in because the sun was completely blocked out by bluish gray smog, a byproduct of the lack of vegetation and emissions from the machines.

Ava stopped abruptly, or at least it seemed so to Myrddin, since he had completely lost any sense of orientation. She motioned to a loose stack of metal panels leaning against each other ahead.

As they stopped, they heard the whirring of drone, which grew louder and higher in pitch. They searched for rocks or bushes to hide under, they found no reliable cover. Their only chance was to continue moving forward and hope to dive into the tunnel in time.

"In here, quickly!" the human shouted, her voice proceeding from a speaker in her helmet, so she sounded robotic herself. She was running as fast as her armor would allow as, the noise of the drone grew increasingly louder. The prince guessed it was just beyond the next pile and that it would crest the top and see them at any moment.

She pointed to the largest panel that had been placed loosely over the others. It was very well camouflaged, hidden in plain sight. If she had not shown him where it was, he would never have noticed the entrance among all the similar piles of lifeless metal. She pulled the covering to one side with her armored hand. The prince noted how, in an environment made mostly of metal, her own metallic covering had certain advantages.

Behind the cover was a small hole, about waist high for him, or about shoulder height for the human. She quickly pulled herself up into it, sliding through in almost one smooth movement. There seemed to be quite a drop on the other side of the hole.

He quickly slipped into the little hole after her, his broader shoulders struggling to fit in the tight space. He barely managed, and slid the panel shut behind him.

"Watch your step," she whispered as she started pulling him forward.

"What is this?" he whispered back once they had moved away from the entrance. At first, he had thought it was simply another hovel which had been formed in the scrap heaps, but he soon saw otherwise. Instead, it was a tunnel, too short for him to stand up straight, but wide enough for two or more to crawl side by side. This shaft was made of stone instead of metal plating. The heap of robot parts appeared to have been carefully placed to conceal the entrance to this tunnel.

The human confirmed all of this for him.

"This is an old tunnel, created by the MoleKind when they still lived in this area."

"I assume they do not anymore," he said, dusting away one of the many cobwebs hanging from the ceiling.

"No, not since the machines took over the area."

"Does that happen often?" he asked. As his eyes adjusted to the dim light again, he could make out more and more. He supposed the human could barely see in this place at all. The bioluminescent minerals which typically ran through the rock formations of Alyrraesia were too small and the distance between them too far to provide useful illumination.

"I guess," Ava said, shrugging her shoulders with little concern. "They are always expanding, always taking up more land, more resources, which means they end up displacing a lot of people."

He shuddered at the thought. If what she said was true, then the Elven kingdom would be in mortal danger. It would just be a matter of time before his home was overrun by the machines and the remnant of his people exterminated. And so it would be for every other living creature on the planet.

"I've noticed over the years that their numbers keep growing, and somehow the armament and technology keeps improving itself, but I've never seen any sign of a leader or a…" she paused.

"A consciousness?" Myrddin suggested.

Ava nodded. "I was just a child when my parents were killed, so I've never understood where these things came from or what they want. All I know is that everybody seems to blame us humans for them."

"Even the finest elven scholars are not completely sure what happened the on day of the Great Change."

"The Great… Change?" Ava asked.

"That's what most races call it. All we know is that a human named James Thatcher led a party deep into the heart of Alyrraesia, seeking to bring magical abilities to your race. He took with him one of the human-looking machines your people called 'robots'. It is said that he was accompanied by a dwarf named Gulthrum Bjornikson and… two elves."

Myrddin's voice faltered at the mention of his sister, but Ava did not seem to notice.

"A dragon seems to have been involved somehow as well, but nobody can tell for certain what transpired. All we know is that all the members of the party all died, and from that point on the machines began to grow, reproducing and improving themselves, and laying waste to our world. Magic also… shifted somehow; dragons grew larger and angrier, races that had been allies for years grew apart with suspicion and blame."

"And humans started turning into rodents." Ava sighed. "Got it."

After an hour or more of crawling, the tunnel opened up into a larger junction, and revealed several tunnels branching in various directions. The ceiling and walls of this section of the tunnel were streaked with veins of the bioluminescent minerals, bathing entire area in soft light, which ranged from amber to green to a bright bluish red. The air smelled slightly damp and Myrddin heard slow drops of water in the distance.

They stood upright and stretched.

"We can rest for a few minutes." Ava said. She detached a red metal cylinder from the side of her armor, spun a lid off the top, and drank from it. She then handed the canteen to Myrddin. He likewise pulled some of the food she had stuffed into his bag and offered it to her. They sat leaning up against the cavern walls.

"Do you have family up there?" Myrddin broke the silence.

He regretted asking almost as quickly as he spoke. The human's face fell, and her tone grew bitter.

"Not anymore, not for a long time."

He began to speak, but stopped himself and simply replied with a silent nod of understanding. He didn't want to pry and upset her, but he was rapidly realizing how little he truly understood about what had happened to the other races since his own people had retreated into their fortress. One of the many virtues the elves had lost since the Great Change and his father's policies of isolation was their curiosity and quest for knowledge.

He waited patiently to see if she would continue on her own without being prodded. Eventually, his patience was rewarded.

"You know many of the races blame the humans for the Great Change and everything which has happened sense. Well, some of them are angrier than others. My parents learned the hard way. They were killed and I barely escaped with my life. I've been on my own ever since."

He stared down at the rough stone floor, his eyes sagging with shame. The Great Change had certainly been a catastrophe, but he was seeing more and more how the responses of blame shifting and animosity might be an even worse one. His stomach knotted at the thought that he was the son of the most spiteful and self-centered ruler of them all.

He whispered, "I'm sorry."

"Don't be. It wasn't your fault," she said, giving him a soothing smile, although he could hear the discomfort in her voice.

"I suppose." He replied. "But I am sorry."

"What about your family?" she asked.

Myrddin grimaced, his mind filling with his dream of his mother's death, followed by his father's rage and rejection. He took a deep breath and answered, still staring at the floor.

"My father is still alive. My mother passed away a few years ago," he said, hoping she would be satisfied with this answer.

"Any siblings?" she asked.

His mind flashed to the portrait of the pale haired Mythria.

"Not anymore."

She cocked her head, taken aback by his answer, obviously not expecting one of the sheltered elves to have also encountered such a loss.

"Okay. Now I'm the one that's sorry," she said hastily.

"Don't be. It wasn't your fault," the prince said with a sad smile. "I didn't even know her anyway. She died before I was born."

They sat and stared in silence for a few more minutes. Each took a breath, as if to start a new line of conversation, then stopped short. Finally, Ava rose and began to re-fasten the sections of armor she had removed when they sat down. She attached her helmet last and spoke through the speaker, her voice sounding mechanical like before.

"We need to cover some more ground if we plan on getting there in time," she said, and reached out a hand to help Myrddin to his feet. They set off through the tunnel directly opposite the way they had come in.

They moved slowly at first but picked up speed as the stiffness wore off. The soft colorful lights of the glowing minerals gave each shaft a unique color pattern.

Myrddin imagined if someone spent enough time in these caves, it wouldn't be hard to recognize each passage individually.

As an elf, he usually preferred the open air, but having narrowly escaped the bleakness of the world above, these passages with their glowing lights and at least a faint feeling of connection to the magic of his world, felt more like home than the barren wasteland he'd recently left.

They rounded a few more corners, and she pointed at what appeared to be a black hole within the already dark tunnels.

"What is this?" he asked.

He put his head into the hole. The lavender light of their current tunnel only lit a few feet ahead. It appeared to be a steep tunnel, almost perfectly smooth. As the light faded, he could see it dipped down and the angle of descent became steeper and steeper until he lost sight of it completely.

Myrddin shook his head as he spoke. "That looks like a pretty steep slide. And we will not be able to manage our speed as we go."

"Down is good, and this will get us going quicker," she said simply. The mechanical voice gave the statement an especially thoughtless tone, which the prince reacted to.

Ava removed her helmet and added with a considerate smile. "Shafts like these were dug by the MoleKind to transport sacks of food and supplies quickly throughout the cave system. It will save time and ensure we won't be followed. "

She was not wrong. He was aware his injury was slowing them down. Sliding down a shaft like this would allow them to cover distance with little effort.

There had to be a catch, though. It was too perfect.

"I assume this is not as safe as I would like," he said, more to himself. But she heard him. And she confirmed it.

"No, It is probably going to be quite bumpy too." She stared at the wound in his side, then up at his eyes.

He met her eyes, then gazed off into the darkness. It grew thick and heavy, making it difficult to breathe the surrounding air. "Oh well, let's do it," he said, taking a deep breath. The wound in his side reminded him of its presence, but there was nothing he could do now. If this would get them there quicker, then he was willing to endure it.

As he prepared himself to swing into the tunnel, feet first, the human's voice echoed through the cavern.

"You know, you're a decent person, for an elf, that is." she said with a wry smile.

He replied as she donned her helmet. "Thanks, I guess. You are the nicest human I have ever met," he said. She had already attached it and slid down the shaft before he said to himself, "The only one, but the nicest."

As he spoke, it occurred to him that this human, this woman, had already extended him more kindness and selflessness than most elves he knew, or anyone else. The exception, of course, being Bayard and his loyal friend Evakhan. He smiled briefly at the idea of the four of them meeting one day and telling war stories of mugs of ale.

Another look at the blackness of the shaft snapped him out of his imagination. Without another word, he slid in.

Chapter 7

The wind rushed past Myrddin as complete blackness surrounded him. Even his elven eyes were not sensitive enough to pick out details in the dark. So, he closed them and hoped for the best.

When the tunnel tilted further down, he could feel all of his organs rise up in his belly, not able to keep up with the rest of his body. He struggled to keep calm. Several times his body left the rocky surface beneath, each time landing with a sharp bump which made the pain in his side feel like he had been punched with a dwarven hammer.

Of all the unnatural, unnerving, un-elfish sensations he'd experienced since he left his fortress, falling out of control in pitch blackness through the bowels of Alyrraesia was the most terrifying yet. All sense of control or connection was gone, and the constant jolts of pain kept him from concentrating long enough to gather his composure.

The only reassurance he had that he was not plummeting to his death was the fact that this human woman had jumped in before him. It surprised him how much he had come to trust her in the few scant hours since they'd met on the battlefield.

The tunnel curved sharply to the right, then up and to the left. His body spun around and his back slammed against a rock. His side sent a wave of pain through him like lightning. The healing had used on it earlier had not been sufficient to prepare for a beating like this.

Eventually, the tunnel ended rather abruptly, and he landed with a painful thud on the floor of a slightly larger cavern. As soon as he was able to move, he grabbed his side and struggled to catch his breath. Myrddin had spent a lifetime hiding any fear or pain for the sake of his people, but at this moment he was visibly shaken.

Ava had already had time to stand up and remove her helmet. She looked down at him with compassion.

"Are you okay?" she asked.

He nodded slowly. The bioluminescent minerals wove through this cavern in thick bands of magenta and yellow, so both the elf and the human were able to see clearly.

"That wasn't as bad as I expected!" she exclaimed with the glee of a child who had just ridden a tree swing or had a refreshing raft ride down the rapids of a river.

"Good," he nodded, still trying to catch his breath. He could not help but wonder how bad she had thought it was going to be if that had not lived up to it. Myrddin also realized her armor, lack of injury, and familiarity with the situation had given her an entirely different perspective than his.

She seemed to realize this as well. "Everything still okay with your wounds?"

He looked down at himself. His tunic was soaked with sweat, and he thought sensed a dribble of blood down his side, but he ignored it. Or rather, he denied it.

"I think so, but it is difficult to tell in this light," he said, as dispassionately as he could.

"If you're talking about the wound on your side, I think it's opened up slightly," a strange voice spoke up.

The prince instinctively rose and drew his sword, albeit not as swiftly as usual. The enchanted blade emitted a faint glow which brightened the surrounding areas thoroughly, but he still wasn't able to make out where the voice had come from.

The human had also drawn her rusty blade in one hand, and her spinning saw in the other, and was looking back and forth around the room, ready for battle.

When they saw nothing more for several moments, the prince spoke up.

"Reveal yourself... please." he stated plainly, lowering his sword, but not sheathing it. He did not want to appear to be hostile, and his training in Elven courtesy had taught him not to provoke a stranger without cause.

The prince's eyes grew wide, and he barely caught his jaw before it dropped in amazement at the being who approached him.

Emerging from a shadowy portion in one corner of the cave, a furry creature came forwards. It was about two heads shorter than the human, with small, white eyes on its somewhat oversized head, and a snout with large gray whiskers which twitched constantly as it spoke. But it was its hands which drew Myrddin's attention the most.

They seemed to have been normal human or Elven hands at one point, before all the muscles of the fingers fused together to create larger, thicker paws with long nails which formed powerful-looking claws which glinted in the light.

All of this, combined with the surprising humanoid features on the creature's face, and the simple human clothing which covered its body, made it a rather grotesque sight.

Though he had never seen one in person before, the prince knew from pictures in Elven books he was facing one of the MoleKind.

Their ancestors were humans before the Great Change. They had long since retreated to the caves to escape the retaliation of the other races. Over the years, living so close to the magical heart of Alyrraesia, magic itself had changed them to better suit their chosen environment, until only the slightest hints of what they had once been remained.

"Who are you?" asked Myrddin, making sure his sword, although still out of its scabbard and easy for him to use if need be, was not pointed directly at the creature.

"My name is Benja, of the MoleKind," the creature greeted in the formal manner of the elves, raking Myrddin by surprise as it placed both claws at its sides and bowed as low as its drastically shortened legs would allow it.

"I can tell you are MoleKind," growled the human beside him. Her own weapon was placed directly in front of her, in a gesture of open hostility. She moved to stand between the creature and the prince, but he reached out to hold her back, giving her a stern glare.

She glared back at him, seething. For a moment, looked like she might turn the sword on Myrddin. Their eyes locked coldly for a moment, then Ava relented. She stepped back, sheathing her dagger. Her spinning blade powered down with a descending whirr.

"Greetings, Benja of the MoleKind. I am Myrddin of the Elves," he said, bowing his own head respectfully to the little creature. The prince had discerned that, if he had ill intention, this odd being could have attacked them each when they first landed and were vulnerable. Instead, he had waited until they had their bearings before making his presence known. This level of courtesy was rare in this world of strife and contention, and the prince decided it was worthy of consideration.

While Myrddin had caught his jaw from dropping at the first appearance of this MoleKind, the words that followed from the creature's mouth next were so shocking, his jaw fell wide open of its own accord.

"I know who you are." Benja replied. "The centaurs told us to expect you and to offer you any help we could." His voice was high and raspy, but he spoke with the grace and bearing of an elven sage.

His surprise grew as the full realization sunk in. This little creature had been sent by the centaurs. And it knew who he was.

He glanced over at Ava. He suspected when the little creature said it knew who he was; it was also saying it was aware he was a prince.

He regretted his decision to hide his royal identity from Ava, realizing that from now on, the revelation might make her doubt his honesty, wondering what other secrets he was keeping. But he also enjoyed being in her presence without her knowing who he was. She treated him as she would have treated any other elf, which was already complicated enough.

"You received a message from the centaurs as well?" He asked.

"Yes," Benja said quietly, "they told us of the elf that would come soon and how we needed to assist you however you need us. But in the manner of the centaurs, they did not say why or give more details. Certainly not that you would be... accompanied." He said, turning to Ava.

He looked the robot clad woman up and down evenly as he spoke, without malice, but also without deference or fear of the armored stranger who was at least twice his size.

"Why magical creatures like the centaurs speak to you, and why would you follow them? Your people have done nothing but hide and scheme for centuries while the real humans stayed on the surface and suffered!" the woman burst out with indignation. Her hand moved toward her dagger, but she did not advance. She just stood, seething down at the MoleKind.

Benja stared up at her blankly and cocked his furry head to one side.

As Ava fumed at him, the realization sank in, and she understood the answer to her own question.

Even before the Great Change, the centaurs would not communicate with a human under any circumstances, as they were a non-magical race, unworthy of their attention. For them to give a message to the MoleKind meant they no longer considered the MoleKind to be human. Instead, they had become a magical race of their own, completely separate from what the humans once were, and in the eyes of the centaurs, superior.

The little MoleKind had been processing the irony of the situation for years, but it landed on Ava like a boulder that had fallen from a high cliff.

The humans of the past would have killed for the opportunity to have magic, to become magical creatures, like most of the other sentient races of Alyrraesia. But none of them imagined getting there this way.

"We may have changed because of the mistakes of our ancestors, and others," Benja said, nodding knowingly to the elf, "But we are now magical creatures just like any other."

Ava drew a heavy breath and looked like she was about to shout at Benja, but Myrddin intervened.

"I understand what you are saying MoleKind Benja," he started, addressing the creature with the respect that it had shown him yet again, "but please understand if my colleague and I are wary considering the experiences each of us have endured as a result of the Great Change."

"I understand," he replied calmly. "I have been chosen from among my people to guide you and assist you as we see fit, so I will help both of you in whatever way I can."

The prince turned to the human and stared at her questioningly. The MoleKind was giving them a choice, either to accept his help or not. The prince knew exactly what the outcome of this situation would be. After all, if the centaurs had seen it, then it would come to pass, just like his own visions.

"I want nothing to do with that..." the human started, shouting so loud it reverberated through the cavern. Myrddin cocked his head and winced angrily at the noise, which stopped her. The little MoleKind did not react, though the prince was certain the sound was even more uncomfortable to his sensitive ears.

"One moment if you would please," he said to Benja, as he turned away, grabbing Ava by her dagger hand and pulling the human a few feet deeper into the cavern. He assumed the MoleKind would still be able to hear them, but at least they would have the appearance of privacy. "We need to talk."

Once they were some distance away, he released her hand and looked at Ava sternly, crossing his arms across his chest.

"Oh, don't look at me that way," she exclaimed loudly enough that Benja and probably any other creature for miles down the shaft could hear. "I understand how you're all high and mighty trying to help all the other races, but now you want to associate yourself with one of those... things?" She waved her hand toward the MoleKind, gesturing to it as if it were a rat they had tripped over in the cave.

"A being such as he might say the same of you, Ava of the humans," he scolded, emphasizing his last word to remind her of her own race's reputation and pain it had caused her.

Her mouth was already open, with an angry retort loaded and ready to fire. But she took his meaning and stopped herself.

They looked at one another in silence for a moment. Ava's armored torso rose and fell heavily as she took a deep breath. Her narrowed eyes softened slightly.

"Fine," she said eventually. "But if this turns out badly, don't say that I didn't tell you so." She pointed her metal gloved finger at him, as if she was trying to at least reclaim some of her dignity by pretending that she was only relenting to please him. But she failed. He had already turned back toward Benja.

Instead, his eyes just softened as he quietly said, "Thank you."

"Very well," she said, still trying to sound harsh.

Myrddin and Ava returned to the little creature, knowing that he had heard everything. Benja simply smiled politely and said, "How may I assist you?"

"We need to locate a refugee camp called as 'Last Chance'. Can you help us find it?" Myrddin asked warmly, as if the recent argument had never happened.

Benja took the queue and replied in a similar tone.

"Of course," he said in his quiet voice, and with a slight bow. "I know this place. I would be honored to help you, Myrddin of the Elves."

Something in the bow and his voice eliminated any doubt from Myrddin's mind. The MoleKind definitely knew he was the prince of the Elves.

"You have my thanks," Myrddin exclaimed with a guarded smile. "Let's get started then."

Ava snapped her helmet back on and started off down the tunnel to the left, as Myrddin and Benja watched. She had gotten several steps down the shaft when MoleKind cleared his throat and said, "Not that way. This way is better."

Benja turned to the right and started walking, with the prince close behind.

"That is going the wrong way," Ava exclaimed as she turned and tried to catch up with them.

"It is," the little creature allowed nonchalantly, "but it will come very close to another tunnel that will take us directly there, as the crow flies, the people on the surface like to say." The prince smiled at the rodent, who smiled back. While his teeth were sharp, crooked, and rather gruesome, the sparkle in his eyes was warm and engaging.

"So you're saying you will connect the two tunnels for us?" Myrddin asked with interest.

"These don't only look pretty.," Benja raised his shiny claws and ducked his head with a modest smile. "They have a purpose, and I am quite adept at using them if I do say so myself."

The prince smiled again. But even though Ava's face was obscured by her helmet, he was certain she was not smiling.

"Seriously?" she demanded through her helmet in her robotic voice, grabbing Myrddin by the arm and turning him around to face her. "We just met this... person."

The helmet jerked to one side. He assumed she was giving the MoleKind a sideways glance. "How do we know we can trust him? He could be trying to delay us, or leading us into a trap!"

Myrddin gently removed his arm from her grasp and tilted his head at her, motioning for her to remove her helmet. She did so, revealing the very expression he had imagined.

"I'm choosing to trust him as I chose to trust you." He declared with growing impatience. "The centaurs spoke to him and obviously told him much about me. He could have already done us harm if he had so chosen. You said you would accompany me until I got to Last Chance. If you would prefer to go on and turn around now, you are free to do so."

She stared back and forth between the elf and the MoleKind with her arms crossed and a frustrated scowl on her face.

"You need to decide, though. Your point about being delayed is valid. I need to continue on my mission either with or without you." The prince said evenly.

She took a few breaths before turning to the side of the cavern that Benja had said they should take.

"Lead the way," she snapped at Benja, as she clamped her helmet back on.

Chapter 8

Benja led the group through tunnels for quite some time, guided by the veins of glowing mineral which lined the passageways. Ava's metal boots clunked along the stone floor, accompanied by clicking and scratching from the clawed feet of the MoleKind. For Myrddin, the trek felt like an eternity. The wound in his side protested all the way.

The MoleKind stopped abruptly and turned to the left before pulling out his claws and sharpening them against each other. He took a second to sniff and tap on several sections of rock, as if searching for the ideal spot to begin. His nostrils pulsed and the whiskers on his long snout vibrated, almost like a hummingbird about to take flight. Myrddin and Ava stood back and observed, fascinated by the creature's odd appearance and habits.

An elf or human would have needed several days and heavy tools to make any progress in the thick stone walls of these caves, but Benja's powerful claws sliced through the stone as if it were made of soft clay. Within moments, he had created a hole in the shape of a new tunnel shaft, similar to the one Ava and Myrddin had slid down earlier. He leaned into the hole to dig, and within a few seconds, his feet disappeared down the shaft.

A few minutes later a call rang out from the other side. Myrddin felt a gust of fresh air waft through the new shaft and motioned for Ava to take the lead.

"Ladies first, as the humans say."

Ava climbed in and the prince followed. The tunnel was a little narrow for his liking, and his sense of claustrophobia was not helped by the human's metal feet kicking his face, but in a few moments, they were through and emerged in a larger cave again.

"Perfect," said Benja, as he pointed to his hole. His face beamed with pride at his workmanship.

"A ha," the prince said, glancing back the way they had come. He saw the other side clearly, but if the MoleKind had not dug the hole, he would never have been aware of this tunnel through the thick stone walls. "That was a lot easier than expected. You weren't joking when you said they ran close together."

"I wasn't," Benja said, shaking his head confidently. "As I said." He crossed his short arms with their long claws across his chest and gave another of his sincere, albeit gnarly, grins.

The prince chuckled as he admired how adamant the little creature was. Turning to the human, he commented, "You see, we make a good team."

"Maybe," she grumbled.

They walked briskly for a little while, everyone quite pleased with how quickly they were getting on their way, when without warning, Benja came to an abrupt halt, almost causing Ava and Myrddin to crash into him. The rodent cocked his head to one side, hearing something none of the others noticed.

"Why have we stopped?" Ava whispered.

The little MoleKind was silent for a few more moments, as the prince joined him in his listening, but Myrddin heard nothing.

"There is something else in this cave," the little creature whispered, his voice barely discernible in the silence.

The human searched around with a confused expression as the Elven prince closed his eyes and focused his concentration, reaching out with his inner perception of the magic and life around him.

"What do you mean?" she asked.

"Something else is in here," the MoleKind replied, "something dangerous."

Benja anxiously shifted from one leg to the other, and his whiskers oscillated nervously. Until now, the rodent had displayed a grace and tact which was totally out of step with his awkward appearance. But now his jittery, hopping and twitching displayed a level of tension which spread to the human and the elf.

Finally, Myrddin sensed the presence of the being Benja had heard.

"It's this way," the prince pointed further behind them, into a larger tunnel which branched off from the one they were in.

Benja gasped in surprise at the prince. "You are right. It is."

"What are you two on about?" the human asked, irritated. She obviously did not appreciate being left out. "Something in this cave? How can you tell?"

"Magic," Myrddin said, while Benja at the same time said, "Vibrations."

The elf and the MoleKind chuckled at their simultaneous reactions, but their faces quickly returned to looks of concern. Ava scowled and shook her helmeted head.

"Have you ever felt anything like this before?" the prince asked Benja, still focusing his magic, trying to gain a clearer view of the unknown creature's location and threat level.

"Only ever at a great distance," the MoleKind said. "And it's always been confusing."

"Why do you say that? " Ava asked. She had drawn her weapons and was staring at the tunnel Myrddin and Benja pointed toward.

"It's more like a clattering than the sound of footsteps, as if the creature has eight legs." the little mole mumbled. His snout was scrunched up and his whiskers were vibrating.

The comment made Myrddin's blood run cold. He instantly withdrew his magic, which he realized would only lead the sensitive, deadly creature towards them.

"Arachnid," he said.

Ava glanced back at him, confused, while Benja's tiny eyes widened in fear.

"What?" she asked.

"I've read about them in the old books from the Elven libraries," Myrddin panted, hurrying them along the passage in the direction they needed to go. "They look like giant spiders. Their fangs are so big they can go straight through your head and come out the other side. Their venom paralyses their prey, but does not dull the pain. So, anyone who is caught by the beast feels everything while the creature devours them."

The little MoleKind nodded in horrified agreement. "My people have had many unpleasant encounters with them in the caves." His hopping and twitching manifested involuntarily as he spoke and turned away. "We should move now!"

Myrddin followed as Benja scurried off down the tunnel, Ava following after a second's hesitation.

"Why would there be one in here? I've never heard of them," Ava muttered as they ran, distress clear in her voice.

"They used to frequent the abandoned dwarven tunnels and the catacombs where they bury their kings. The magic in the old dwarven bodies was released back into the ground in high concentrations. That, combined with the cozy tunnels, were perfect for them to lay their eggs and make a nest in," Myrddin spoke as quietly as possible, given their pace. He hoped the human caught all of his words, or at least the important points.

"It's getting closer! Benja cried out.

He was correct. Now the monster was so close Myrddin discerned its position by hearing. He knew the Arachnid could do the same. "The can sense the vibrations in the air and earth like you can. We will not be able to outrun it."

"So now what?" the human asked.

The prince's mind raced through his classes. He tried to recall everything he had learned about the Arachnids and their tendencies. He knew how vicious they were and how unlikely their survival would be if they had a direct altercation. Arachnids were suited for areas like this, born to hunt in underground tunnels. Elves and metal-clad humans were not. Fleeing was their only viable option.

"What does this tunnel do up ahead?" he asked Benja.

"Not much," the creature managed between pants. "As I said, it is straight for a long time, with a few slight bends."

"Any narrow spots?"

The creature was quiet for a moment. "One, maybe narrow enough, but it's far away."

"Then we had better run," Ava shouted as the gigantic spider creature entering the tunnel behind them. The clicking of its feet on the stone resounding through the cavern loud enough for even the human to hear clearly.

Myrddin's ever-growing list of non-elf-like terrors was growing larger by the second. He was being chased in the dark by a creature so terrifying that he dared not turn around, and which was getting closer by the second.

The corridor narrowed, but not enough, and they all knew it. Unless something changed drastically, they would not survive the next few minutes.

Benja struggled the most. His body was not built for speed. His weight was held too low, his legs too short, and his heavy claws weighed him down. He used them to grasp the sides of the cave walls that were closest to him, digging his long nails in and propelling himself forward in an attempt to move faster. This helped a little, but not enough.

Myrddin turned his head when he heard the MoleKind's cry of despair and saw that his new comrade had fallen a little behind them and was nearly in the clutches of a terrible beast. This was the prince's first sight of an arachnid in person, and he considered that the drawings in the Elven books did not give proper justice to how fearsome and repulsive this monster was.

The arachnid was as tall as a horse. Its body was covered in a strong, wiry hair, so thick and stiff that it managed to scrape the stones off the walls before bending. The prince imagined those would be like steel daggers against the skin of another creature.

The mouth was easily visible behind its fangs, which were as long as a human arm. Its face was covered in glassy, black eyes, looking in every direction, constantly scanning and observing. The eyes were hungry and eager, as if the creature had just been served the juiciest meal. Which the prince supposed, the beast imagined it had.

"Faster, it's gaining on us!" Myrddin shouted to Benja. But it was no use. The beast had almost caught up with the MoleKind. The Arachnid had even opened its mouth to prepare to devour the rodent, revealing its giant fangs, dripping with paralyzing venom. If the MoleKind was even grazed by those, he would be dead. The spider slowed, preparing to pounce.

Benja looked to the prince with horror and desperation in his tiny eyes. Although Myrddin was too focused on escaping the Arachnid to reach out with his magic, the terror coming from the soul of the rodent radiated into his own soul, as did the malice of the giant spider.

Without another thought, he dug his heels into the ground, and spun around. Since the Arachnid and Benja were still hurtling towards him, he covered the distance between them in less than a second, pulling his sword from its sheath as he lunged. The enchanted blade glowed pale blue in the dark caves.

The elf and the Arachnid pounced simultaneously. They met in the middle; the creature's mouth landing on the glowing blade, stopping the teeth less than an inch from the MoleKind's head.

"Run!" Myrddin shouted at the MoleKind and the human.

Benja did as he was told, running toward the human. Ava stopped running and turned, having missed the action that had happened within the past few seconds.

The Arachnid pulled its mouth away from the sword and shook its bulbous head with a high-pitched scream.

Myrddin wheeled around and set himself and his sword into a battle stance. His mind and body had reset themselves from fleeing to fighting, and his years of training took over. He evaluated the monster, not as a childhood nightmare, but as an enemy on the battlefield with strengths and weaknesses, like any other. He swung his sword upward as the creature's pointed teeth reached for his body, and then again, and then again.

The arachnid attacked in rapid succession, striking like a viper with its teeth while throwing distracting blows with its two forward legs. Myrddin parried the blows, but the Arachnid moved too quickly for him to make any offensive strikes.

The exertion wore him down. His side was wet with fresh blood and his head was growing foggier by the moment. His arms grew heavy. He struggled to lift their weight, never mind the weight of the sword that they tried so desperately to hang onto.

He considered calling forth a magical attack, but it was too late for that. Both his mind and his limbs were wholly focused on the physical battle. There was no opportunity to concentrate, much less to chant or cast. The beast seemed to sense that its prey was growing weary, as did all of the amusing snacks that dared to put up a fight before they were devoured.

The spider reared back and raised its head and forelegs to make one last strike. The prince had barely enough strength left to raise his sword in a futile attempt to block the attack, when the sound of spinning blades went whizzing past his head. He instinctively ducked to avoid the noise. When he glanced up, he spied Ava's makeshift blade weapon digging into the Arachnid's exposed torso. Black ichor spewed from the monster's body, and it reared back with another loud screech.

"Run! That won't stop it for long!" Ava shouted through her helmet as she too turned to run, taking advantage of the beast's pause to examine its injury.

In the distance, he noticed a pile of rocks that created a narrow pathway that he knew the Arachnid could not pass through. He only hoped that the rocks were solid enough that they prevented the creature from moving them.

"This way!" Myrddin shouted, pointing toward the tunnel with his glowing sword .

They sprinted down the tunnel. In the dim light, Myrddin observed that Benja had already passed the pile of rocks and was waiting for them.

"Benja!" he shouted. "Make sure those rocks will hold! If that thing gets through that we all die."

His feet ached as they pounded hard against the stony cave floor. With every breath, and every step, his side sent searing pain through his entire body.

He grabbed the human by the arm as he passed her, pulling her along, trying to give her the momentum she needed to prevent the Arachnid from catching up. As he ran though the cave, filled with pain, numb from exhaustion, and dragging the armored human, the world appeared to dissolve into slow motion and he found his mind clearing.

He remembered stories of such things happening to those who were at the brink of death. His thoughts wandered to his sister, the princess. What would she have done in a situation like this? What were her final moments like? Did she experience the pain he was feeling? Was she afraid, or did her mind clear and drift to memories of her own?

He wondered if his father would receive news of his death like had received news of hers. Would the king become even more sullen and withdrawn at the loss of his remaining child? Or would he receive the news with indifference and simply reckon that he'd been right all along about his son's foolishness and incompetence?

But then he thought of the other elves. Those he smiled at when he passed them in the hallways, the children he often played with, Evakhan who had so desperately wanted to accompany him on his journey. He might not be missed by his father, but he would be missed. And for that reason, he needed to live. His people, and possibly others, needed him to keep going.

This thought, and the fact that he had reached the rock crevice, snapped him back to reality. He almost didn't fit, and the rocks were very solid, not moving at all, he realized as his body squeezed through. He dragged Ava in behind him. Her armor scraped against the walls of the hole, dislodging a few loose rocks as she scrambled in. Benja stared at the crevice with concern, hoping their shield hadn't been weakened.

Ava landed with a loud thump but scrambled up instantly. She yanked off her helmet to catch her breath. As she did, Myrddin beheld the terror in her eyes as the Arachnid charged toward them, sticky black goo still oozing from the wound Ava had inflicted.

All three of them stood back several paces from the crevice and waited, hearts pounding in their chests, as the beast approached, its legs scraping and scratching the stone on the sides of the narrowing tunnel, its teeth chattering and grinding against each other with the screech of fingernails on stone. It wouldn't do much good to keep running as the creature had proved it could outrun them.

The beast ran headlong at the narrow opening. A few more loose rocks fell from the ceiling and rolled away, but the crevice held. The Arachnid took a few steps back and tried another full-body assault with similar results, and this time it appeared to wince in pain from the oozing hole in its torso. Then the spider tried a new tactic. It braced its hind legs against the floor and walls of the cave and picked at the sides of the crevice with its forward legs. It dislodged several individual stones, and the hole got bigger. The beast tilted its multi-eyed head from side to side to survey its progress.

Myrddin tried to muster the power to cast an offensive spell, but he was too exhausted. Ava considered drawing closer to use her blade weapon, but she would have needed to reach through the crevice, too close to the Arachnid, which would have been much too dangerous. As she and Myrddin watched the Arachnid picking away, they suddenly saw it jump back in pain from a rock that had flown past them and hit the creature.

The gigantic spider roared and screeched louder than ever, causing Ava and Myrddin to wince at the sound.

They then turned around to observe Benja's sharp teeth bearing a satisfied smile. While magic spells and mechanical blades were useless, an old-fashioned thrown rock was just enough of a distraction to give the monster a second thought. Such an attack wouldn't do much damage to a healthy Arachnid, but perhaps a tired and wounded one would be a different story.

Ava and the prince immediately joined in and threw loosened rocks through the crevice at the spider, aiming for its head, its mouth, and its wounded torso. When they ran out of rocks to throw, Benja used his claws to dig into the side of the cave to provide more ammunition.

The monster tried to ignore the onslaught and continue picking, but several of the rocks landed on their fragile targets. One shot of Ava's caught the torso wound, which opened wider. The black ooze increased.

The prince both saw with his eyes and sensed from the Arachnid's intense magical presence that their attacker was losing its interest in its prey.

As Myrddin and Ava continued their assault, the rocks that hit the creature landed in front of it and formed a pile that made progress more difficult. At last, the monster became tired and crept away. The group listened as the scratching and clattering of its huge frame gradually diminished as it left this section of the caves. They were safe for now.

The party listened in silence for a long while as they caught their breath and allowed the realization that they had not died to settle in.

Finally, Benja broke the silence.

"The wound on your side has opened up again," he whispered.

Myrddin glanced down at himself. He could barely make out a small patch of shiny liquid across his side. It was blood.

He shook his head. "We need to keep moving," he said as he wiped it away and stood up to go. "This will be the least of my worries if the Arachnid changes its mind and figures out how to get past that barrier."

The rest of the party nodded in solemn agreement and they proceeded down the tunnel with Benja leading. They continued at a brisk pace for many hours, only stopping to rest when absolutely necessary.

After some time, the tunnels widened, and the lighting became brighter. The veins of glowing mineral in this section were a fairly consistent shade of light blue. The waves of glowing blue in the stone ceiling and sides of the cave gave the impression that they were walking through clouds on a dreamy moonlit night. In another situation, it might have been beautiful, even romantic. But right now the light was simply allowing them to see so they could move closer to their destination and further from danger.

As the party entered an immense chamber with several tunnel branches, Benja stopped abruptly and started sniffing and twitching. He placed his hands and ears against the wall of the cave. "They are above us," he said in a whisper.

"What? Another one of those spider monsters?" Ava asked, reaching for her dagger.

The MoleKind shook his head. "No. The machine army. They are above us."

Myrddin calmed himself and reached out with his inner sense to confirm this. As he allowed his consciousness to reach further and further up through the ground, he found what he was looking for. It was not a connection to the life energy of the machines, since they had none. What he felt was an overall sense of tension, fear, and death as the plants, animals, and living beings above him ran for their lives or were destroyed.

The prince shuddered as he drew back within himself. "I think you're right," he said, nodding to Benja.

"I can't 'sense' anything, but if that's the case, we'd better stop standing around here and get moving then," said Ava impatiently.

The prince shot her an annoyed glance, but his face softened. He wondered how frustrating it would be as a member of the only non-magical, sentient race in the world.

Even before the Great Change, humans had been considered inferior by most of the other races because of their lack of magic. The humans had tried to compensate by creating machines that could move and some that could almost think. Others had attempted to gain magic for themselves, usually with disastrous consequences. After the disaster, the reputation of the humans had gone from bad to worse.

The prince wondered how much of the current turmoil was really the humans' fault, and how much responsibility was on the shoulders of the other races.

The pain in his side snapped him out of his thoughts again. He examined the patch of blood. It had dulled slightly, not looking as shiny as it had before. He hoped that meant that the blood had coagulated and that he would not be losing too much more of it. He could not afford to be weak and he did not know how soon he might have time for another healing spell, much less the availability of the necessary herbs.

They moved quickly and quietly, more slowly than before, as they were all exhausted. The tunnels seemed never-ending. In some places, they would widen , in others they would get narrower, but it was all the same. The prince was convinced they were going in circles, the rock on all sides looking so similar in the pale blue light.

Finally, Benja stopped at the entrance of a long, straight tunnel whose walls were pitch black. The only light was a dazzling glow coming from the tunnel's exit far ahead. Myrddin and Ava stared at each other curiously. Benja simply smiled at them, turned, and led the way in.

They emerged from the dark tunnel into a rock ledge that formed a balcony, overlooking a gigantic cavern whose walls were of green and brown stones, and whose ceiling was streaked with blue and white bioluminescent minerals. Their glow was accented by an enormous circle of pale gray light beaming from the center. As Ava and Myrddin's eyes adjusted to the relative brightness from the previous tunnel, they each had the sensation that they had somehow suddenly been transported back to the surface in the middle of a moonlit meadow.

Benja smiled as broadly as his narrow snout would allow and pointed to the far side of the enormous room.

As their eyes and their attention cleared, they saw where the MoleKind was pointing. Far on the other side of the cavern was a giant steel door.

Myrddin gazed around in awe as he followed the MoleKind through the room. The cavern's ceilings were so high, and the sides so wide they might have fit the entire Elven city in it. He had not realized it, but he had felt an ever-increasing pressure on his chest as they had gone deeper and deeper underground. This vast space gave him a feeling of lightness, like a weight had been lifted.

As they followed Benja through the vast cavern, He glanced over at Ava, who had removed her helmet and was also gazing in wonder at their surroundings. "Dwarves?" she asked.

The prince nodded. Only the dwarves would have had the skill or the interest to create such a marvel so far beneath the surface of the world. As they surveyed the faraway door, they saw it was as tall as a house, and had the shine of high-quality dwarven steel. But more interesting than the door's size or construction was a thin sliver of light that was pouring out from around the door's sides.

At first, Myrddin thought he was imagining it, but Ava spoke up.

"You see that too, right?" she asked, blinking her eyes. "I've finally got enough light to actually see, but now I'm wondering if I'm hallucinating!"

"Yes, the light is definitely there," Benja replied with a knowing nod. His tiny eyes were even smaller from squinting and were covered by his thick brows.

"Where are we?" Ava asked, taking another look around the cave. Her eyes were wide with wonder and, for the first time since the prince had met her, her smile was not forced or sarcastic. It was genuine and lovely.

Myrddin turned to look at her and caught himself gasp. The way the light caught her face made her seem ethereal. With her helmet in her hand, her dark hair fell across her shoulders. The blue glow from the ceiling brought out the blue in her eyes. In this light and with this expression, her features were both strong and elegant. She was stunning, even among elvish standards.

Perhaps it was the fact that she reminded him of Mythria. At least, how his sister had been portrayed in the portraits that he had seen of her. Whatever it was made his breath catch in his throat. Fortunately, her attention was directed at the surrounding room, and then at Benja, waiting for an answer. The prince recovered his composure before she glanced in his direction.

"We have reached the underground entrance of the dwarven cavern of Kasselheim where the refugee camp you were looking for is." Benja replied with a bow and a sweeping motion toward the massive door.

"This is Last Chance?" Ava asked, amazed. "How did we get here so fast?"

The elf and the MoleKind chuckled at each other, earning a dirty glare from the human. Ava pulled back her arm like she was going to smack him, but she considered his injury mid-swing and pulled her punch.

"It's amazing how much ground you can cover when you're going mostly downhill with a giant spider chasing you." Myrddin replied with a warm smile.

"I believe you humans call it... adrenaline." Benja added.

"Oh, okay," she said. It might have been his imagination, or the lighting, but Myrddin could have sworn that her cheeks became pink. He tried to suppress another chuckle at her embarrassment but failed. She was about to take another swing at him when the MoleKind intervened.

"This would be a good place to rest for a short while." Benja said. "The journey to the door is further than it appears from here. The passage behind us was deliberately made too small for an Arachnid to get through. Once we have rested, then we can make our way down and see if we can get anyone on the other side of the door to answer."

"I'm fine, let's just go." Declared Ava.

While the underground surroundings, with no sun or stars, didn't give any indication of time passage, Myrddin imagined they had been travelling for well over a full day without rest. But Ava had almost hit him twice, and he wasn't eager to test her again. So glanced to the MoleKind for confirmation.

Benja bowed his head and replied humbly. "My apologies. While you are both mighty warriors, but I am a simple cave dweller. I don't believe I have the strength to go on without at least a few minutes' rest. Please forgive my frailty."

Ava nodded with a frustrated sigh and sat down. The prince shot Benja a quick smile of appreciation. Myrddin also seated himself with his back against the wall of the balcony. Within moments, the elf and the human had both fallen into a deep sleep under the watchful eyes of the MoleKind.

Chapter 9

When the prince awoke hours later, Ava was still asleep, and Benja had disappeared. After a brief moment of concern, he looked around and saw they appeared to be safe. He assumed the MoleKind had scurried off on an errand, or was scouting the area ahead, like one of his comrades might do during a hunting party.

Myrddin used the period of peace to examine his injury. The wound was continuing to heal, but slowly because of the previous day's exertion. He slipped into his meditation position and began his healing chant. He made some small progress before the chanting awakened Ava.

"How long have we been asleep?" she asked groggily. "And where is the MoleKind?"

"I do not know the answer to either question." The prince replied. "There is no sun or stars to track the passage of time. And Benja was not here when I awoke. Surely you are not still suspicious of him?"

"I'm suspicious of everybody, and old habits die hard." She replied flatly. "Especially old habits that keep you alive."

Myrddin shook his head and looked away. As he did, he watched Benja scurrying up the stone stairs which led to the floor of the room below.

"I trust you are both feeling better after a bit of rest." The MoleKind said graciously.

"Where were you?" Ava demanded. "And don't think I don't know what you were up to, talking about how tired you were. That was just a ruse to get us to rest."

"Rest, which we desperately needed and were too proud to admit." Myrddin added. "You did us a kindness, Benja."

"You both give me too much credit." The rodent insisted, ducking his head. "I was certainly exhausted as well. As soon as you fell asleep, I made a quick survey of the area to make sure we were safe. Afterward, I slipped down to the cavern floor and found a corner where I burrowed a hole to sleep. We MoleKind prefer to sleep in tight spaces, not large open ones like this."

"How soon will we to reach the door?" Myrddin asked.

"The door looks closer than it is and descending to the floor level will take time as well. We should leave as soon as you are ready." Benja replied.

As they made their way further into the cavern, descending from the stone balcony, Myrddin realized the place was much larger than he had thought. The construction of the walls and floor played tricks on his eyes. While the door looked like it might be only a few paces away, as they walked, the door appeared to remain the same size, never getting bigger, never coming closer.

Myrddin remembered an adage one of his tutors had taught him. "When you can't trust your physical senses, use your magical ones." He closed his eyes as he walked and stretched out with his mind but found nothing but air. He pulled and pulled his magic, as if stretching on a piece of string, trying to pull it as taught as possible.

As he reached the outer reaches of his range, he finally made contact with the door. The metal appeared black in his mind, separate from the surrounding stone and devoid of any life, but he 'saw' several seams of color running through it: deep blue, purple, and a gold that shimmered and sizzled. Not only had the dwarves made this, but the elves must have enchanted it, apparently to deter enemies or thieves.

After what felt like an eternity of travelling, the door grew larger before them.

Up close, it was bigger than he had imagined from his first glance across the cavern. It was taller than a house, almost the size of a castle. This close to such an enormous structure, he felt the enchantments which radiated through it. They had been weakened by time and he couldn't discern their exact purpose, but they were there.

He pulled his sword from its scabbard. Slowly, he raised it up and used the pommel to knock on the door.

Three steady knocks.

The sound swelled and echoed through the cavern like a war gong. Benja covered his ears and winced at the noise.

"I'm sorry, my friend, but that's how these old dwarven doors work." The prince advised. "The sound carries the knock and alerts those on the other side that someone is requesting entry. In the old days, a request would be met swiftly. But in these times the refugees may be too afraid to answer."

They waited a long time, but no reply came. He tried reaching with his magic, but the enchantments on the door not only blocked his abilities but gave him a throbbing headache when he tried.

He raised his sword and repeated the knock over and over. At about the tenth round of banging, the human spoke up.

"The fools aren't going to let us in!" She shouted. "We've risked our lives and come all this way to help these people, and they won't even talk to us! Now the robots are going to wipe them out and we'll either get killed by the machines or one of those spider monsters. I knew I should have stayed in my workshop."

Myrddin shook his head, ignoring her rant.

He raised his sword up again and banged hard on the door. He wrapped both hands around the hilt of his sword, raised it over his head, and came down upon the door violently from a high angle.

A tumultuous boom reverberated through the cavern, immediately followed by a scream of pain from the elf. He dropped his sword and fell to the ground, his right hand torn and bleeding.

Ava rushed to his side. "Are you alright? What was that? What happened?"

Myrddin breathed heavily and gasped with pain as he replied. "Ugh. I should have known better!"

"Known what?" Ava demanded.

Benja replied as the prince struggled with his injury. "One of the dwarves' ways of keeping intruders away. It's an optical illusion. Quite brilliant actually."

"What are you talking about?" Ava shouted, moving to inspect the circle of Myrddin's blood which dripped down the face of the door.

"The surface of the door appears to be flat when viewed at eye level. But in truth, it is constructed of tiny needles of the strongest steel, all pointing upwards. The effect is made complete by an elven enchantment." The elf answered. "I can feel shards that have broken off inside my hand. The enchantment and rust must have worn the surface down over the years."

The human looked at him in concern, "Are you alright?" she asked quietly.

He took a deep breath before answering. "I will heal. Just don't touch the door with your bare hands."

He paused for a moment, focusing his magic on his hands, and only his hands. It was almost as if the rest of the world faded into darkness around him as his eyes shut slowly, but his hands remained bright in front of him. They glowed an odd blue, similar to his sword. He observed the areas where his blood, far brighter than the surrounding flesh, spilled out of the areas surrounded the deep red of the steel needles.

With a single pulse, he tried to attach the end of his magic to each of the foreign objects in his palms. There were hundreds of them. He deduced from all the red flecks which the metal had been extremely brittle and had shattered into millions of pieces with the force he had put into them.

He grabbed as many of the larger pieces as he could and moved his hands downward with a single motion.

The magic had held the larger pieces in place, as he had willed it to, like a magnet of magical particles. As he moved away, he extracted most of the pieces. Opening his eyes, he inspected a bloody glob, with thousands of gray specks suspended within.

He moved them off to one side before he 'dropped' them.

"Be careful," he said to the human, as he looked at her gloved hands. The metal of the salvaged robot parts would definitely be stronger than the needles. "Your gloves should be fine, but make sure you touch nothing else."

Ava placed her hand on the prince's shoulder. "Step back a minute, let me try something." She turned to Benja, "You're gonna want to cover your ears."

As Myrddin knelt beside Benja and comforted him, Ava put her helmet on and adjusted a few knobs on the side of her armor. There was a low hum, followed by a high squeal from a speaker embedded in the helmet's mouth. Ava leaned her body against the giant metal door, pressed the speaker against it, and shouted at the top of her lungs.

"Let us in! We have important information! You are all going to die!"

Both Myrddin and Benja cringed as the steel door reverberated with the sound, shaking the whole cavern like an earthquake. The words repeated several times as they echoed off the walls of the giant cave. They were answered by a chorus of more echoes as the sound travelled down the shafts of the connecting tunnels.

The word "die" lasted for several seconds, and finally faded away.

Once Myrddin and Benja recovered, they stared up at Ava, who had turned off the speaker and was removing her helmet.

"Well, if that doesn't get their attention, nothing will." She said wryly.

The first thing the elf noticed wasn't the door moving, but the shaft of light changing shape ever so slightly. It was so slow he thought it was his imagination at first. They were opening the door. Just a crack, but it was all he needed. He grabbed his sword and shoved it into the gap which had formed between the two doors.

Cries and shouts came from the other side. The prince heard grinding noises and felt the pressure on his sword increase, but the enchanted blade held fast.

"Wait, we don't want to hurt you. We come bearing news of the surface. You are all in great danger. You need to let us in!" Ava shouted, directing her speaker into the crack.

It was silent for some time, and then sounds of loud discussion broke out on the other side of the door.

Eventually, someone came forward and replied.

"Who are you? And what news have you brought us?" the voice slipped though the tiny crack in the massive door.

Myrddin could not help but breathe a sigh of relief at the voice. "I am a messenger from the elves. Along with me are my companions, Ava and Benja. A robotic army is headed your way. You need to vacate immediately if you are to stand any chance of survival."

He listened to more murmuring from the other side followed by silence. They had decided amongst themselves, whomever they were.

Slowly, the enormous gates eased open further, the hinges groaning under the colossal weight of the steel and the rust which had gathered due to disuse. When it was cracked open barely enough for one person to walk inside, it stopped.

The voice from the other side spoke again. "We will allow entry to the messenger. Your companions must wait outside until we are convinced of your story's truth."

"Agreed." Myrddin shouted as he slipped through the tight passage.

Once on the other side, he heard a gasp. Or rather, a collection of gasps. He smiled knowingly at their expressions. They had not been expecting him to be an elf. The elves never left their fortress. When he had spoken, they had thought either he was lying, or if he was a messenger from the elves, but of a different race. He certainly had their attention.

As the door creaked closed behind him and Myrddin's eyes adjusted to the new surroundings, he estimated the room they were in was as large as the cavern outside, if not larger. The ceiling was covered with collections of large rocks which shone so brightly they appeared to be like several small suns inside the cavern, shining light down on everything below. If the previous room had been a moonlit evening, this area was lit like a blazing desert.

It occurred to the elf that this lighting scheme was both attractive and defensive.

If attackers were somehow able to reach the previous cavern, and somehow get past the colossal doorway, their eyes would be lulled by the softness of the previous cave and then blinded as they entered this one. It was clearly the result of a combination of elfish enchantment and dwarfish ingenuity. He thought about his father, the King of the Elves, holding his royal court in a dark storage closet, and he longed for the days when the races cooperated well enough to create such marvels as this.

He also noted several dozen balconies nearby in the walls at varying heights, which had been clearly intended as battle positions for archers and spell-casters to defend the doorway from invaders. The prince imagined there were several great containers above his head which might be used for pouring flaming oil or some other violent liquid on the heads of unwelcome guests. But the balconies were not full of warriors or wizards, just a few shoddily clad, terrified looking refugees.

His marvel turned to pity as his eyes lowered and he surveyed the buildings and beings in front of him. All around them, they viewed tents, huts, and other scant structures made from scrap wood, quickly thrown together. While the construction of the individual buildings was slipshod, they were organized to create streets and alleyways much like a town.

The illusion of experiencing a sunny day involuntarily caused the prince to draw in a deep breath. But when he did, the stench almost knocked him over. Excrement hung in the air along with the smell of old sweat and disease. He imagined the people inside had gotten used to it and probably did not notice anymore. It was disgusting, but he understood these creatures had no other choice. This place was called 'Last Chance.' for a reason.

The people that were gathered there surprised him, too. There were few of them, probably only about fifty or so, and they were in various states of disarray. Some of them had bandages on various parts of their bodies, others had missing limbs.

He recognized the sallow hues of disease and infection in their faces. But what surprised him most of all was the diversity of the group.

Most of the residents were dwarves and MoleKind, which made sense in the underground setting. But to the prince's shock, he beheld humans as well. Not the changed humans, distorted over the years, but actual humans, like Ava.

Perhaps more surprising and tragic, were a few dryads. Myrddin shuddered to think what it would be like for such free-spirited woodland beings to be trapped in a putrid setting like this. Their race loved the trees and was bound to them, more than the elves, with whom they'd having always been friendly, but without ever getting involved in any formal alliance. The dryads had been the only race which could completely claim innocence in the Great Change, and they had been one of the least affected, too.

Each of the able-bodied creatures held a makeshift weapon in their direction, making sure the prince did not travel any further into the place than what was necessary. All except one dryad, who looked up and down at the elf thoughtfully. This single dryad was about the size of a regular human but with a little horn, similar to that of a young deer, and leaves instead of hair. She stepped forward to represent those around her.

"Why would the machine army be coming here?" The green-tinged tree spirit spoke. Her voice was soft and calm, but Myrddin knew enough of the tree spirits to know that, when separated from their trees their emotions were volatile and unanchored. They had a reputation for becoming dangerous without warning and he did not want to anger her.

"I honestly do not know their motives." The prince replied sincerely. "This may be their target or they may trample this place on their way to somewhere else. My companion Ava and I tracked them heading in this direction a few days ago and we've journeyed here to warn you."

"I see." The dryad said in a somber tone. She turned and whispered to a small committee composed of one member of each of the races represented in the room. After conferring for a few seconds, heads nodded, and the dryad returned. "We will now speak to this companion of yours." She waved her hand, and a creaking noise filled the room again as the door reopened.

The entire makeshift city erupted as Ava stepped through the doorway. Those with weapons raised them, and those without weapons ducked for cover. She had put her helmet back on to squeeze through the narrow entrance, so she was in full robot array.

As the citizens were getting ready to attack her, Benja squeezed through the door as well and stood in front of her, waving his tiny arms. "Wait! Stop! She is not a threat".

The would-be attackers paused, seeing a member of a race with whom they were familiar. That gave Ava enough time to remove her helmet and raise her hands with her palms open. The refugees lowered the tools and farm implements but continued to stare are her warily as she joined Myrddin.

"This is one of the newer dwarven tunnels." Benja said calmly. Having partially recovered from the assault to his senses.

Myrddin himself had been wondering about that. But with Benja's words, it instantly made sense.

"It is thousands of years old," one of the humans, an older one-armed man, interrupted.

"Yes," Myrddin nodded, "but the dwarves had only started on it when times changed. There are still a lot of valuable metals in the soil here that which not been mined out, and a lot of tunnels to allow for easy access to those metals."

The dryad held up her hand, silencing the mumbling crowd behind her. At her gesture, not only did the disorganized murmuring stop, but they also raised their weapons, which had slowly started to droop, up high again.

"These people mean no harm. We should treat them as honored guests as they have come a long way in order to bring us news. Let us gather around a table so we might give them some food and water." She said softly, her eyes meeting the elf prince's. "My name is Cedar. Welcome to Last Chance."

"Your offer is most gracious." The prince said with a humble bow. Food and water would be one of their most precious resources. For these people to share it with strangers or newcomers was an act of sacrificial kindness.

Cedar's eyes widened, and she gave a nod of recognition at the prince's act of humility. Dryads had a similar lifespan to the elves and many similar customs. This dryad, probably old enough to remember the times before the Great Change, would understand that elves bowed their heads to no one but the Elven king.

While the dryad led the party and talked to the prince diplomatically, the other residents eyed them with mixed expressions, especially Ava. And none of the inhabitants of Last Chance put away their weapons. Myrddin noticed they carried them naturally, as if everyone in this place felt the need to protect themselves on an ongoing basis. Whether that resulted from their perilous journey to get here, or a sign that Last Chance was unsafe, was unclear.

"I thought the dwarves buried all precious things with their kings in the catacombs. Why wouldn't the machines go after one of those?" Ava whispered to Benja as they were led toward the large table made of a single slab of stone in the center of the encampment.

"Precious gems, yes," Myrddin replied to her quietly, but loud enough to show their hosts they weren't hiding anything, "and soft metals such as gold and silver, those are treasured by the dwarves, but useless to the machines. They are seeking the solid stuff; iron, copper, tin, and other metals to make more robots and drones. Unfortunately, this camp is right in front of something the machines would consider a gold mine."

Ava's eyes widened. "The door!" She exclaimed as she pointed to the giant portal through which they entered. "Their metal detecting sensors have probably been attracted to it from miles away. It would be like a beacon to them."

Murmurs bubbled through the crowd. Refugees nodded, pointing at the door and at the newcomers.

"Exactly." The prince replied. "The dwarven craftsmanship and elven enchantments were designed to keep away living intruders, arachnids, bandits, enemy armies. Machines with the ability to think and destroy were not even in the worst nightmares of the artisans who built this door, and I don't know if it will hold for long once the machines take over the area."

They arrived at the large table and remained standing until all were in place. Cedar nodded, and they all sat down. Several MoleKind, small for their race, appeared and placed small bowls before them, each containing a grayish porridge with pale yellow lumps which appeared to be a root of some sort.

Again, the entire company waited until all had been served. There were no utensils, so Myrddin and Ava looked around, then looked at each other, wondering what the table etiquette was for ingesting the food. They expected such hungry creatures to jump at any available morsel, and the fact that everyone waited politely was remarkable.

The elf and the human's astonishment at the refined culture of Last Chance was mitigated somewhat as the dryad nodded, and all of those around the table picked up their bowls with both hands and poured the porridge down their throats. The exception was the MoleKind, who stuck their snouts into their bowls and slurped up the stew, making a clicking sound with their tongues and teeth. Most of the dwarves threw their bowls back so greedily that drips of gruel and bits of the pale root drizzled down their beards.

Myrddin and Ava looked at each other, nodded in appreciation again to the dryad, and ate their meal. Fortunately, they were so hungry, it actually tasted better than it looked.

Unlike elfish or dwarfish feasts of old, which lasted for days, consuming such a small portion only took a few seconds.

"What are we going to do then?" the dwarf across the table from Myrddin asked in a gruff, tired voice. His rusty, dented sword was lying in his lap, unsheathed, and his hand never got too far from its hilt.

"We need to get out of here as soon as we can," Myrddin said. Many of those around him nodded in agreement, as did the dryad, who was so obviously in charge, but there were a few who appeared to be hesitant.

"And where will we go?" asked one of those, a human. "When they are finished here, the drones and robots will go somewhere else if we escape without them noticing us."

Myrddin could hear the hopelessness in the speaker's voice, though he did not see who it was, and he could see those feelings spread through the crowd as quickly as they had tumbled into existence.

He sighed softly. "While your questions have merit, they are growing closer and closer with every second. We have little time to discuss."

One of the older human women replied angrily. "There is nowhere for us to go. And, if what you say is true and they are making an army, we will not have much world left soon, anyway. Is there any point in moving on?"

Nods and murmurs of agreement rolled across the room.

The prince shook his head in frustration. He looked to the dryad at the head of the table, who stared blankly at him.

"What other choice do you have! Aren't you listening? Use those brains inside your head. You are all going to die if we don't leave now!"

Myrddin and the rest of the room all jumped at the outburst, and turned to see Ava standing up, pounding her fist on the table. The metal-clad fist on the stone table made an impressive gavel, and the sound got everyone's attention.

All around the room, hands reached for weapons. Creatures stood and gathered into clumps, some looking ready to fight, others ready to run, and still others clinging together out of fear.

The dryad, however, remained seated and simply raised one leafy eyebrow.

Rising slowly, and speaking as kindly as he could, Myrddin said, "Ava. Please do not be angry at these people." He turned to them all as he continued. "We understand this place has become your home. Some of you were born here and know no other life."

"Think of days long gone when the creatures could walk through fields and forest with no worry from the machines. Of the days when children could play, and food was plenty. Of the day when mother and fathers grew old and died soundly in their sleep or lived long enough to see the children of their children," he met the eyes of those few that had young children with them.

"I know this is not possible now. But if we stay here and die today, it will never be possible. By moving on, we at least have some sort of chance of experiencing that in the future. The journey will be difficult, but we will find somewhere to go."

He had barely finished before the same dark-haired dwarf who had spoken up earlier spoke up again. "And what do you know of that, elf? Your people abandoned the rest of us a long time ago," he spat at the prince. "Perhaps if your people were not so cowardly, maybe we would have been able to defeat the enemy a long time ago and we wouldn't be here!"

Nods and rumbles erupted among the dwarves and dryads, spreading through the room.

Myrddin had been afraid the reputation of the elves would eventually catch up with him. He took a deep breath and looked the dwarf in the eyes.

"I understand your anger, but I do not believe you fully understand the reason why the elves have hidden."

"What do you mean?" The dwarf demanded.

"Master Dwarf," he started, "allow it to be heard from your plainspoken mouth, and not from mine, so the people may know it is true. How long do elves live?"

The dwarf spluttered for a moment, unsure where this was leading. The dryad stood and answered in the creature's stead, crossing her arms and smiling knowingly. "About twice as long as a dwarf, I've been told. And I think dwarves should be able to get to about five hundred years if they make it to their old age."

"My understanding is," Myrddin corrected, "dwarves can live to about eight hundred years, or at least they were before the world changed. An elf, though, lives about two thousand years."

"So there should be many of you to help us," exclaimed the dwarf.

"One might imagine so. But how do elves have children? I would appreciate your input again, kind dwarf."

Yet again the dwarf spluttered, not expecting the question. The elf prince waited patiently for him to answer, or for someone else to step in, in his place. But none answered. He glanced over at the Cedar but she just smiled warily, watching the exchange play out.

The room became quiet. Myrddin paced as he spoke, making eye contact for a few seconds with each creature in the room. He saw fear and anger, but he also discerned curiosity and inklings of compassion. Finally, a human male with white hair and beard, wearing what might have once been a uniform of some sort, spoke up.

"When an elf reaches their thousandth birthday, they are allowed to approach magic and ask for a child. They only receive one if magic permits it. I know nothing of the specifics or rituals involved, as the elves keep such things to themselves, but I'll say I learned this from a reliable source."

Myrddin nodded slowly to the dwarf, confirming his words. "Only in our thousandth year, are we able to have children. And again, one hundred years later. In rare cases, does magic grant any requests for children after that, or before. For this reason, the elves have all but died out."

At this statement, a fresh wave of murmurs swept through the room. The prince waited patiently for the quiet to resume. "The Elven king does not wish the rest of the world to know it, but there are only about a hundred elves left." Myrddin bent his head. He had betrayed his father, betrayed his king, by giving out that information and weakening the position of his people. He knew he would suffer for it later. If not at the hand of the king himself, at the hands of his own conscience.

But he had no time for recrimination, so he continued, "That is why he retreated into the heart of the mountains we once lived around. We did fight, but unlike the rest of the races, we could not replenish our numbers. For the first hundred years of this war, we were butchered. We may have magic, but we die the same as the rest of you. And we are now facing extinction."

The crowd grew hushed for a moment as residents looked at each other and back at the elf. But the silence was quickly broken.

"Then why did you come all this way to save us?" the belligerent dwarf bellowed. He could see the dwarf did not even believe his own argument anymore. He did not want to be proven wrong in front of the rest of the group. "Why did the king not stop you?"

"Because" Myrddin started carefully, "I could not allow the rest of the world to die while I sat around, waiting for the day I was married and was old enough to approach magic to ask my wife for a child."

The prince looked around the room. The crowd was splitting into factions. Some, mostly humans and MoleKind, were looking at him with sympathy and approval, nodding their heads, energy building. Others, mostly dwarves, frowned and nodded in agreement toward the dwarf, shaking angry fists and pointing fingers in the elf's direction.

Myrddin looked to the dryad. He watched her survey the room and saw her brow furrow with concern. The prince smiled as she stood to speak, but his blood ran cold when he heard her words.

"You have told us much, yet there is one thing you have left out. Tell us your name, elf."

"Why do you ask that?" he said, trying, and failing, to evade the question.

Instead, her eyes hardened. "The elf king was once a kind man, accepting of all the races, even the humans, but after the change in the world, and the death of his then only child, the princess Mythriya, he changed. He became a hard and cruel man, bent on preserving the few remaining elves at all costs. He would never allow one of his warriors to leave on such a mission. What is your name?"

He remained silent, not wanting to lie, and not being able to answer the question.

Ava glared at him, throwing her hands up in confusion. He could see the questions flit through her eyes. He had told her his name. Why was he being so weird about telling these people?

"His name is Myrddin," she declared in an annoyed tone.

The green-haired creature jumped to her feet. All those around her raised their weapons to prepare for fighting, but she held up her hand again, halting them. The room became so quiet that everyone could hear her whisper as she looked Myrddin in the eyes. "We are not in the presence of a common elf." She raised her voice and declared, "We are in the presence of the Elven prince, the heir to the throne, the son of the Elven king."

Everyone except Benja let out a gasp as the weight of the information struck them. The dwarves and dryads all dropped to one knee and bowed their heads while the humans and MoleKind looked around with confused expressions.

"I am no prince," he shouted, walking in circles and waving his arms. He approached the chief dryad and offered her his hand, inviting her to stand.

"Are you not Myrddin, crown prince of the elves?" Cedar inquired as she rose.

"I am Myrddin," he nodded, "son of Dalen and brother of Mythria, but I am no prince. How can I be a prince when the Elven nation no longer exists, and my father longs for the daughter who was taken from him all those years ago?"

"But you are still his child," the dwarf from earlier said, "and his second one at that. If something were to happen to you, he would not be able to have another. There is also a rumor that the queen is dead." The creature's eyes, previously filled with anger and rebellion, were now filled with a look of awe.

Myrddin nodded yet again. "It is true. My mother is dead. She died in a terrible accident when I was only a child. And elves do not remarry."

"So if you die, the Elven nation will truly be without hope," Cedar said calmly, her eyes analyzing him. Her expression said she believed him, but was trying to understand why the prince make such a decision. "They will have no king in the future. They will fall apart. The elves have always been under the leadership of the king and the council."

Myrddin smiled sadly at her and shook his head. "And they will survive under the leadership of the council if the worst happens. But if I do not do what I can to protect this world against the machines, then they will not survive at all."

The dryad locked eyes with him for a long moment. Then, without looking away, she declared loudly, "We will leave this place under your guidance, Prince Myrddin of the elves. If you think that is best."

Her voice left no room for argument or discussion. Even the troublesome dwarf nodded his head respectfully at the prince and crossed his battered sword across his chest in a dwarfish salute.

"I not only think that it is best, I think it is the only viable option we all have. And we need to move quickly."

"Very well," the dryad said, before she stood, shouting out commands for the people to prepare themselves for departure. They gave each other grave nods, and each attended to their duties.

Chapter 10

T he dryad called her council together, and after a brief discussion, they all dispersed and started giving instructions to the residents of Last Chance.

Myrddin returned to Benja and Ava. The human was standing with her hands on her hips and a stern frown on her face. "Why didn't you tell me you were a prince?" She challenged.

He gave a guilty shrug. "You did not ask. And I did not think it mattered."

"Well, it sure matters to them! And you might have let me decide if it mattered to me or not. You're the future leader of an entire race!"

"Perhaps I am. Perhaps among my people, I am their prince and their only option for a future king. But I do not rule the humans, the dwarves, the MoleKind, the dragons or any other race. Having my title made known might even make me a target for other races who hate the elves and would seek to destroy us. That belligerent dwarf is not the only one who feels betrayed by my people."

She stayed silent for a moment, as they watched the people scurrying along, trying to gather the few possessions they thought were important enough to take with them.

"Is it true what was said about the life span of the elves?" Ava asked.

"Yes," Myrddin answered, warily.

"How old are you?"

"Far older than you." He said with a smile, trying to shrug off the question.

"How old are you, Myrddin?" she insisted.

He sighed. "I am almost three hundred years old, little more than a child amongst my people."

She laughed, "But older than I'll ever be."

"An elf's life span is both a blessing and a curse," he explained. "We live far longer than a lot of the other races, except perhaps the centaurs and the dragons. Dragons can live for tens of thousands of years, and nobody knows much about the centaurs. We know we have a lot of time in this world to do many things, but we also watch our friends grow old and die around us."

She sat quietly, a variety of emotions fluttering across her face before she eventually whispered, "I'm sorry."

"Don't be. It is how elves are. As you cannot help how long the lifespans of humans are." His voice was matter of fact, but his eyes were sad, and he turned his face away from her.

"I'm twenty, by the way," she said after another moment.

He opened his mouth to reply, but they were interrupted by a tense looking Benja. He was drumming his claws against each other, and his snout was twitching.

"Myrddin," he whispered, "I can hear them growing closer, we're out of time."

The prince nodded his head, standing to approach the dryad who had finished packing her own meager possessions.

"Where are we going to take these people?" Cedar asked. "We are few, but a most are ill or injured. Many will need help and won't survive a long journey."

A young dwarf standing nearby spoke up.

"Prince Myrddin, if I may?" he asked.

"Yes, speak." the prince said. "But first give me your name dwarf."

"My name is Droran Magnusson, Dwarf of... nowhere," the creature said, bowing his head in shame. The elf knew dwarves were proud of their homes and clans, and would include their specific caverns in their titles. For him to have no home to name would be seen as a disgrace amongst his own kind.

Myrddin smiled to himself. "Greetings Droran Magnusson," he said, clapping the young dwarf on the shoulder, "Dwarf of Last Chance."

The dwarf's eyes grew wide as he realized what Myrddin had done. The Prince of the Elves had given him a name. A proper one too, suited for a dwarf. His eyes glistened. He looked up at the Myrddin with appreciation, then turned his head down again, but this time with a broad smile.

The prince simply nodded as he continued, "Now, what input have you? We must hurry."

"Thank you, my prince," the young dwarf said, bowing his head in thanks. "These people are not fit for a long journey. But we may not need to go far to avoid the creatures who approach."

"What do you mean?" the prince asked thoughtfully. "Do you know of a place we can take these people?"

The dwarf nodded his head furiously. "The ground surrounding these caverns are filled with minerals the machines need. Dwarves never mined them, as they were too close to these grand halls. We just need to move far enough away from this area for now, perhaps to chambers the dwarves have mined clean. Or perhaps chambers that are filled with items which are useless to these creatures."

The prince glanced at the others. Benja, Ava, and Cedar all nodded with approval.

"Well spoken, my young friend. Do you know of such a place?" he asked, eager to leave as soon as possible.

The dwarf bowed his head again. "I am afraid not, my prince." he admitted. "I was born in this chamber and lost my parents when I was young. I have never ventured far from this place, and have not had the courage to explore a lot of the surrounding caves. But I imagine if anyone would know, he might," the dwarf pointed to Benja, who appeared surprised to have been considered by the other creature.

"What do you think, Benja?" asked the prince. "Do you know of anywhere down here that is close enough to move these people out of danger?"

The little MoleKind's eyes narrowed, and his whiskers twitched in concentration. Then his eyes brightened and widened. "Actually, I think I might. But there is a problem."

"What is it?" Myrddin asked.

"I must admit I have never been there myself," the little creature said. "I have only heard of it, and it does not have a reputation of being safe."

The prince nodded his head in understanding. "We have little choice at the moment, Benja. We need to move and move now."

"Understood." He said, looking back at the doors to the chamber from which they had entered. "I need to connect and widen some tunnels. Get everyone out of this cavern into the next one and close the door once they're clear."

Benja and Myrddin looked at the dryad, who nodded with approval.

"Everyone, into the cavern," the dryad called out, her voice ringing through the entire cavern, projected by her magic. "Those who are able-bodied assist the sick and injured. Bring nothing with you. The steel will attract the robots, and everything else will weigh us down. Move now!"

Benja ran to the door as Myrddin, and Ava moved to the mechanism which opened it. Myrddin reached toward the giant wheel, but glanced down at his right hand, which was still shredded from the door's trap. He shrugged at Ava.

"I've got this." Ava said as she reached up and turned the wheel as the mighty door creaked open. Benja squeezed through as soon as there was enough room, and Ava paused while the others gathered in groups and prepared to leave.

"Well, would you look at that?" She marveled as an elderly dwarf carried six tiny MoleKind children in his arms, the furry creatures squirming and tugging at his gray beard, while their mother limped beside them on one leg.

The prince pointed at two dryads who were holding the hands of a blind female dwarf and speaking encouraging words to her as they led her toward the door. "This truly is amazing. I have never seen such cooperation. I just hope we are not too late." He sighed.

Ava turned the wheel and opened the door wider as the refugees started slipping through. First one by one, and then two by two, and finally in larger groups.

She smiled and nodded as they passed, except for one group who drew her up short. They appeared to be a family who had come together as the result of loss. A male with two children who bore a close resemblance to him, and a female with four offspring of her appearance. They were all holding on to each other, older children taking care of the younger, each parent with expressions of care and concern over the entire group. Ava would have found the scene sweet and hopeful, except for one thing.

The female and her children were MoleKind, and the man was fully human.

As the group passed through the door, Ava's eyes met those of the mother's first. Her glare of indignation caused the female rodent to bow her head to the ground at first, but then she gazed at the six children all supporting each other, and her eyes rose to meet Ava's with a satisfied smile.

It was Ava's turn to look down in shame.

When she raised her head again, the mother and children had passed through the door and the father was standing, waiting to meet her eyes before he exited. In less than two seconds, they had a conversation with their eyes which conveyed an entire lifetime of regret, forgiveness, and hope. Then, he smiled through the door at his family and rushed to catch up with them.

Ava turned to Myrddin, wondering if he had observed her interchange with the family, but his eyes were closed and he was chanting softly, the way he did when he was reaching out with his magic.

"Are you... sensing... anything?" Ava asked.

Instead of replying to her, he spoke with urgency to the remaining residents, "Everyone, hurry. They have entered the first layer of tunnels. Move quietly."

The last few people hurried toward to the door. Only Cedar and the young dwarf remained. "Ava," the prince started, knowing she would disapprove of what he was going to ask of her, "I need you to move all these people into the tunnel Benja is digging without delay. We'll follow you as soon as we can."

"But..."

"We have no time for discussion." He said as he drew his sword from its scabbard. The faint glow of the blade shone in the dim light. "Take this," he said, handing it to her by the hilt. "The light will guide you and the rest of the people. "Are you sure?" she asked, her face covered in shock.

"I cannot use it now," he said, pointing to his injured hand, "but if I need a weapon, I will find something around here, or use my dagger."

She stared at him for a moment, wanting to protest, her chest heaving up and down slightly, but she relented.

"Alright," she mumbled, uncertainty clear in her voice.

She took the blade gently from his hands before turning away and moving toward the door.

"Dwarf Magnusson, will you assist me in closing the gates behind the last people?" he asked the young dwarf in a tone that was more of a request to a valued colleague than an order from a royal to an underling. The dwarf nodded frantically. "I would be honored to serve beside you, my prince," the dwarf replied enthusiastically.

"Just Myrddin is fine," he smiled.

"Then I insist you call me Droran," the dwarf grunted.

"Very well, Droran," the prince laughed. "I doubt the machines will follow us. I think it's the door itself they're after, but we cannot rely on that. We need to close the door from this side, but we don't want to trap ourselves here. Any ideas?"

The dwarf examined the huge metal wheel with wooden spokes, which opened and closed the door mechanism. It was embedded in the wall near the door and was taller than Myrddin. He paced back and forth between the mechanism and the door, looking them up and down and rubbing his beard in concentration.

"I reckon a door this size would build up some mighty momentum once you got 'er going. We'd need to open it much wider first, pull hard to get it moving, then dive through at the last minute just before it slams shut." Droran considered.

"That's a sound plan, my friend. Risky for sure, but a sound plan indeed." said Myrddin.

Myrddin stuck his head through the door to the other cavern. He could see the faint glow of his blade bouncing away from them, down a shaft some distance away. When he came back into the room, Droran was drawing his foot against the floor of the cavern, making a line in the dust with his boot.

"I think if we open it this far, we should be able to build up enough momentum for the door to carry itself closed long enough for us to dive through. You'll go first and then I'll follow you." Droran explained.

"I am thinner than you, and able to run faster. You will go first."

"As you say." The dwarf replied with a slight bow.

They ran to the wheel and started to pull. Myrddin could reach higher but only had partial use of his right hand. The little dwarf found that he got the most effect by jumping up and grabbing a spoke while it was yet above his head, and then using his weight to ride it down. They soon developed a rhythm, and the mighty doors gradually eased open.

Myrddin reached out with his mind to find the machines, only to run into them faster than he would have liked; the black holes that they left in the otherwise magically rich and colorful environment of bright reds and oranges impossible to miss. They were only a few tunnels away from them and moving briskly.

"We need to go faster. The gates are not going to close in time. The robots should not be able to make it, but we risk one of the drones getting through."

His mind drifted to the robotic creatures, slipping through the air at speeds that even an elf could not match on the ground. Their high-pitched whirr haunted him.

"Don't worry," the dwarf said confidently. "I won't let the slimy little bugger through. Just keep pushing pri... Myrddin. We'll make it."

As the door neared the mark on the floor, they indeed found that it had built up enough momentum to carry itself several inches. It ground to a halt a few inches past the mark and Droran jumped up to pull the lever in the opposite direction.

The prince reached out with his magic again. He reached his tendrils into the surrounding caverns, making sure that he saturated every crevice with them, as if he were flooding them with water.

He did not have to scan far. "One tunnel away!" He shouted.

Only a moment later, the nightmarish whirring sound echoed through the massive chamber as the first of the drones entered, followed immediately by a swarm of others, all flying in perfect synchronization.

They were divided into several squadrons, which each moved as one unit. Their formation reminded Myrddin of the flight of geese; a triangular arrow cutting through the sky. The first three fanned out in opposite directions, surveying the room.

The prince and the dwarf heaved on the door with all of their strength. Myrddin even used his battered right hand to gain a little more speed.

He watched as one of the drone squadrons paused in midair and spun in their direction. Then the other two squadrons followed suit. After a second, all three squadrons sped toward them as several more entered the cavern, accompanied by speeding robot tanks on track wheels.

"We have to go!" the prince shouted as the dwarf landed on the ground from his last ride down the wheel. Droran ran to the door and pulled his sword, waiting to make sure the prince was following before he exited.

With a loud cry that was half grunt and half scream of pain, Myrddin pulled the level down with both hands and ran toward the door. The dwarf barely squeezed through the rapidly diminishing opening and the elf dove through behind him.

Falling out onto the floor on the other side, he shot a glance back to see the door shutting behind him. The door closed with a bang that reverberated throughout the cavern, followed by several even louder ones as the first squadron of drones slammed into it.

They both laid back on the ground for a moment, covering their ears as the noise echoed throughout the cave and wandered off down the connecting tunnels.

As the sound died out, the dwarf burst into a fit of hysterical laughter, which the prince could not help but join.

When their bellies ached and they were gasping for breath yet again, the prince finally spoke up.

"That was far too close for comfort."

The dwarf just chuckled again, and in typical dwarven fashion, commented, "Now that was exciting."

The prince chuckled again, although he instantly regretted it as his body reminded him of his injuries. "Ha, you are a true dwarf indeed. There is no mistaking it, Droran."

"Thank you, Myrddin."

"It's time to go." He said as he got up, dusting himself off and offering his hand to the dwarf. "Sooner or later, the human-shaped robots will arrive and open the door. We need to be as far away as possible by the time they do. Plus, the others will need our help."

The prince was surprised by how fast Droran's stubby legs carried him. Their pace was more of a leisurely jog for the slender elf, but they made it across the cavern without incident.

"I'm pleased to see there aren't any stragglers. It appears all the refugees made it at least this far." Myrddin remarked as they approached the connecting hole that Benja had created.

They saw the hole was quite sizeable and might fit two or three dwarves side by side without them having to bend or touch the sides.

Droran whistled softly as he gazed into the impressive tunnel that had not been there before.

"That little mole sure does know how to dig, doesn't he?" he said in awe.

"He does," Myrddin said, beaming with pride. "He does indeed."

They made their way through the tunnel carefully. It was dark, with only a few random streaks of the lighted mineral, and the floor was full of loose stones from its recent construction.

When they reached the other side of the tunnel, they met an even darker one which curved at a sharp angle. Neither the prince nor the dwarf could see very well in the light and the prince had to use his magic to find stone sides.

Fortunately, as he reached out with his magic, its tendril stretching forward, he found the people of Last Chance. The different colors of light were abnormally bright in the dark cavern, even though they were just in his mind. Reaching out, he gently placed his hand on where he knew the dwarf's shoulder should be, directing him with a gentle nudge. "They've gone this way, not far at all."

They walked slowly, neither wanting to trip on any ridges and needing to regain their bearings. As they walked, the dwarf sighed.

"Sometimes I wish I had magic like the elves to be able to tell things and cast enchantments. But alas, I am stuck with as little as the humans."

"What do you mean, Droran? Elves might be able to reach out and bend magic to their will, but dwarves have it coursing through their very veins."

"They do?" the dwarf asked, shocked.

"Apologies, my friend, I forgot that you have not had many other dwarves around you to instruct you on what a dwarf is, and what they can do."

"Aye, that's a truth. I've been on the run from the machines as long as I can remember. And there wasn't much time for socializing or schooling in Last Chance." Droran said.

They emerged from the dark MoleKind-made tunnel into a natural cave with enough gray-green light for them to see clearly. Stalactites hung from the ceiling and a small stream flowed out of a hole in one side, pooling in the middle and then disappearing on the other side. There were a few scraps of cloth and food wrappings.

"Then allow me to begin your education." the elf replied as they paused to drink from the stream. "Let's start with some of your most basic abilities. Have you ever held fire in your hand?"

"No! I'd prefer not to burn!" Droran snorted.

"But you have never actually burnt yourself before, have you?" the prince asked, hoping that the creature might catch on.

"No, because I'm careful," Droran retorted as if it was the most obvious thing in the world.

The prince let out a little of a sigh. Being hard-headed was another well-known dwarfish trait.

"No," Myrddin shook his head. "You have never burned yourself before because dwarves have skin that is thicker than that of any other creature."

"Hey..." the dwarf started, preparing to retort to what he assumed was an insult yet again.

Instead of answering, the prince pulled his dagger from his boot and threw it in the dwarf's direction. The dwarf shouted as the dagger made impact and then fell harmlessly to the cave floor. Droran's eyes widened.

"See," Myrddin said after the dwarf had retrieved the dagger and realized what he had thrown at him. "You can go into battle without thick armor because your armor is your skin, which covers you entirely. To kill a dwarf, you need to have a weapon with powerful enchantments woven into it, or you need to be a creature with just as much magic flowing through their veins as the dwarves."

Droran picked up the blade and studied it, turning it over in his hands. He touched the tip ever so gingerly with his finger. He pushed a little harder, with no effect. He then proceeded to poke himself over and over, giggling as he went, as if he were playing with a toy.

"Fire," Myrddin continued with a smile, "although a dangerous weapon, is not magical. Dwarves are the best blacksmiths because they can reach their hands into the forges and work on the glowing metal with their bare finger, shaping it more precisely than any other creature ever could."

They were silent for a while as the little dwarf seemed to think about it.

"So would I be able to survive an attack from a robot or a drone?" he asked curiously.

"Not exactly," Myrddin answered.

"Not exactly?" the dwarf asked, sounding a bit frustrated. "But I thought that you just said..."

Myrddin had to cut him off again. If the dwarf started ranting without having all the facts, it would be difficult to stop him, and he just did not have the energy for that.

"Machines are very dangerous, and your skin is not impenetrable, just a lot tougher than any other creature's skin. Imagine that you have a fine coat of chainmail. Does that mean that a robot or a drone will not kill you?"

"No," Droran relented, "the armor can still fail, if it is hit the right way, or if you can get in a gap."

The prince sighed with relief, pleased to see that at least he was not completely unreasonable.

"Exactly. You do not have skin everywhere, Droran. Think of the eyes, the mouth, the nose. These are all your most vulnerable places. And the machines might just get their hands on a piece of enchanted steel without even being aware of it. If that happens, then the weapon is as effective against you as it is against any other creature. Do not let overconfidence be your downfall."

He clapped the dwarf on the shoulder and Droran returned the prince's dagger. Myrddin pointed toward the tunnel across the room, and they set off in its direction.

"How do you know so much about the dwarves?" Droran asked as they both stumbled, the floor having gradually dipped lower. They entered the freshly dug tunnel. This one had just enough purple and orange light to make out the floor and edges.

"The dwarves and the elves have a long history together," Myrddin explained as they walked. "You have always produced such wonderful metals, and we have always been skilled at enchanting. We made a strong pair throughout history and our races were firm allies."

The elf hesitated, unsure of whether he should say more, then continued, "But all friendliness ended after the Great Change a thousand years ago. All I really know about dwarves is what I've learned in books."

They were silent for some time before Droran spoke again. His voice was surprisingly quiet this time, almost ashamed.

"They say it was a dwarf that was partially responsible for all of that. That is why the other races are so reluctant to speak to dwarves."

"The same argument could be used for the elves," he admitted, realizing that he was yet again saying things that his father might consider to be treason.

"What happened that day?" Droran asked.

The prince sighed at the comment, recalling everything that he had read, and all the whispered conversations he had overheard. The king had refused to allow him to be tutored in such a topic, and that had only made him want to know more about it. Especially after he heard his sister had been involved in the events and had been a key player of some sort.

"To be honest with you, nobody is really sure," he said. "We know who went on the journey that caused the Great Change, and we know their reasons. With the help of a few visions from the centaurs that they have been gracious enough to share with the rest of us, we can only make the vaguest connections to try to figure it out."

"Who went?" the dwarf asked, hanging on his every word.

"A human, a dwarf, and an two elves." he admitted.

The dwarf laughed after a moment.

"I don't know about you, but it seems similar to the group that you turned up with," he chuckled. "A human, a dwarf and an elf. Or in your case; a human, a mole and an elf. It sounds like the start of a bad joke."

Myrddin could not help but laugh along with the little dwarf. He was not incorrect. In the back of his mind, he was pleased that the connection had been drawn between himself and his sister.

Finally, the tunnel opened up into another roomy cave, about the size of two or three houses. The ceiling was high, and the light was a dim mixture or reds and purples. But in the center of the room, Myrddin saw a different kind of light. The glow was pale blue, and it was moving.

His sword.

They had found the group.

Chapter 11

In the dim light, Myrddin could make out some faces that he had seen earlier, barely recognizing others. The party seemed to have made it safely, even those who were ill or injured, and had made a camp to allow those who needed to rest temporarily. Clumps of people stood or sat around, talking, resting, and nursing their wounds.

He saw Benja far across the room, having a discussion with the Dryad and the other leaders.

A young dwarf called out to Droran, who went over to say hello. Ava stood, with the sword held high. Her shadowy face was covered with a blanket of relief.

"Are you okay?" she asked as she ran to him, her metal boots clanking across the cave floor.

She threw her arms around him and hugged him enthusiastically. His smile turned to a wince as she squeezed a little too tight for his injured ribs to bear.

"Oh, I'm sorry!" she gasped as she released him.

"Don't worry. I'll be fine." He replied as they walked toward Benja and the leaders. "I'm happy to see you too."

"I'm very glad that you made it out of there alive," Benja said as they approached, his muzzle curling into a sincere smile. "We were getting worried when it took you so long to catch up with us."

"Sorry to worry you," Myrddin said, feeling a slight blush creeping up into his cheeks. "We had an encounter with the machines on the way out, but hopefully they'll be too occupied with the door to bother coming after these people."

"I think you've made a new friend," said Ava mockingly, looking behind him.

He turned to observe Droran, waving happily to the little group, before bidding them farewell and making his way over to Myrddin; a happy little skip in his step.

"Hello everyone!" the little dwarf exclaimed gleefully. "I'm happy to see you again." Myrddin smiled as his human and MoleKind comrades greeted the young dwarf with hearty handshakes and shoulder clasps.

He looked around the rest of the room and slowly shook his head in wonder. Ava approached him, still holding the sword aloft to add light to the room. The blue glow gave her eyes an extra sparkle as she smiled at him and inquired. "Is something wrong?"

He blinked and shook himself out of his thoughts. "No, quite the opposite." She met his eyes and inclined her head.

"Go on... if... you don't mind, that is." She said.

He took a deep breath and replied wistfully. "Until a few days ago, my entire world consisted only of other elves. Other races and creatures were only stories and drawings in musty, old books. "

Ava nodded. "And most of those were suspicious at best, and enemies more likely? Yeah. I get it."

She handed his blade back to him. "I guess you should take this back now."

Their hands wrapped around each other as she passed the handle to him.

"You should keep it," he said, still holding on to the handle, and her hand.

"I couldn't," she said, shaking her head and looking down. "I wouldn't feel right leaving you without a sword."

"I've got the dagger," he said, pointing to his boot.

"It's not the same. Besides, a blue glowing elf sword doesn't exactly match my robot armor." She laughed.

He laughed with her as she released her hand and stepped back.

He took his blade, and instead of returning it to its scabbard, he raised it high above his head. "That's just as well." He said. "It has a few tricks you're probably not aware of."

He took a deep breath, shouted an Elvish command, and flung the enchanted blade into the ground. Its pale blue glow brightened and a vein of blue mineral in the cavern walls began to glow as well, lighting the entire room. The tip of his sword stuck into the ground, kept firmly in place by the hard stone that surrounded it, and allowed the rest of the weapon to stand straight into the air.

Gasps of surprise and approval filled the room. Members of the elder council, who were seated in a corner, nodded with appreciation.

As he turned and back to the rest of the group, the dryad stood suddenly, her green-tinged skin glowing strangely under the light of the enchanted blade.

She met his eyes, as if asking permission, and waited for his nod before speaking to the people that she would probably have spoken to without a moment's consideration before.

"Your attention please," the dryad said, addressing the group of people before her as well as the prince. "We are safe for the moment, but we cannot survive for long here. We have no food, no water, sick people, and we have nowhere to go from here."

The prince nodded to the dryad and looked around the room as if searching for the answer somewhere in the cave walls and tired faces around him. His eyes landed on Benja, whose bushy brows was furrowed in deep thought.

"Benja, you seem to be aware of quite a lot of what goes on in this land; from tunnels to Elven culture the ways of the centaurs. Where did you learn all of this?" he asked.

"I only know about what is happening underground," Benja admitted. "The MoleKind have a method for communicating with one another involving taps, and a language of sorts that the humans used to refer to as 'Morse code' a long time ago. It's like letters represented by a certain amount of taps."

"Would you be able to send a message like this along, asking if other groups are aware of any other refugee camps that we might be able to help these people to join?" he asked.

"Of course," said Benja. "I assume I should also send out a warning about refugee camps being in areas where the dwarves have not completed their mining of the useful ores."

"Please," he said, grateful for the little creature's foresight. "Thank you, Benja."

The mole went off, tapping the wall lightly with his long, sharp nails as he went along. Myrddin stared at him in amazement. He appeared to be testing the sections of cave wall to determine which spot would carry the sound with the greatest efficiency.

Myrddin was very grateful that the centaurs had provided him with the little creature as an ally and tried not to ponder their reasoning behind it. Perhaps they foresaw that Myrddin would need him.

"Not all of us want to go back into a refugee camp," the dryad spoke up, looking around at the able people next to her. The little group had formed and approached Myrddin without him noticing. Some of them were nodding along, agreeing with her fervently.

"What do you mean?"

"We have considered your words, Prince Myrddin," she declared, looking specifically at the dwarf that had been so troublesome earlier, his head now bowed low in shame, "and what you have risked coming here. We wish to follow your example, under your leadership. We will join you in the battle against the machines."

The dwarf raised his head and looked Myrddin in the eye. "You've shown me, elf, that living in hiding has made me soft and foolish." He lifted his rusty sword and shook it angrily. "I'd rather die in battle like a warrior than starve down here like a coward." He looked the crowd over and considered his options. To say that they were not battle-ready was an understatement. They were a handful of tired, undisciplined malcontents whose primary reason for following him wasn't for honor or to protect the weak. They just wanted out of this cave and into some fresh air, even if that only lasted a few days. In a battle, they would likely get in the way and dilute his attention rather than be an asset.

If they wanted to follow him, he needed to lead them with strength and honesty. He took a deep breath and strode around them, looking them up and down like an officer inspecting his troops.

"You understand, you will most likely perish." he said in a commanding tone. "We are outnumbered and have little weaponry. What you are volunteering for is likely a suicide mission. Best case, we will slow the machines down to give those we leave behind a better chance for survival."

Cedar looked around at the others and stepped forward. "We understand." She declared as the others nodded in agreement. "Those of us that have come forward have little else to live for. We do not want to waste our lives sitting by and doing nothing when our sacrifice might mean something. And those of us who have loved ones would rather die trying to make a better life for them than sit by and watch them live the lives that we have been forced to live." Her face hardened at this last statement.

Myrddin met her eyes with understanding. The dryads were a race with a deep connection to their trees. Each dryad was bound to her individual tree, and to her entire forest, with a spiritual tie that transcended bonds of friends or family from other races. They would live in forests and would die protecting them. For a dryad, a life without their tree was no life at all. And if a dryad was out here, that meant only one thing. Her tree had been destroyed. Probably her entire forest.

"I understand," he said, nodding his head slightly. "But we cannot leave the refugee camps entirely unprotected. Some of you must stay behind."

Restless murmurs filtered through the group. He raised his hand to quiet them, then pointed around at the sick and the injured as he continued. "We cannot take all the able fighters and leave the children, the sick, and the injured behind. They will need protection and leadership, as well as scouts, to help them find food, water, and a more permanent shelter."

The frustrated faces of the crowd shifted to a mix of agreement and confusion.

"What do you suggest, Prince Myrddin?" Cedar asked, bowing her head in deference.

He paced around the room for a moment. He passed a female dwarf holding a dwarven baby in one arm and a MoleKind in the other, both cooing and playing peacefully with her dark auburn beard. She looked down at the babies with a warm smile and raised her eyes to the prince. He nodded to her, then turned to address the others.

"You will split yourselves into two groups," he commanded. "Those who have family and loved ones here, and those who do not." Cedar nodded with approval as she understood the wisdom in the prince's strategy. "If you have family here, you will serve best by staying here and protecting them. If you have no attachments, then you are truly ready to risk your life with us on the outside."

"Very well." Cedar nodded with a look of fierce determination and what Myrddin discerned to be... relief. She seemed to be gratified that the prince's plan would allow her to leave the caves and the weight of leadership. "Dostan... Nolet... Siggebela... and Jardolin, you will stay. Come, here is what you'll need to do."

While Cedar delegated the leadership of Last Chance, Myrddin slipped into a quiet corner of the cave. He closed his eyes, took a deep breath, and reached out with his magic to scan for enemies on their path ahead. He sensed the occasional clump of Molekind and dwarves here and there, but no opposing army, at least not yet.

As he pulled out of his trance, he noticed Cedar had dismissed the new leaders and was waiting for him to return.

"We will have to move soon, within the hour. Gather whatever belongings you need and meet back here as quickly as possible.

"We will, my prince," said the dryad, bowing perfectly at the waist. The humans and Molekind nodded as the dwarves bowed their heads and slapped a fist across their chests in salute. They all dispersed with an energy he hadn't seen in the group before.

"I think you are forming a little army here," Ava joked quietly when they were far enough away to not hear anything, nudging him lightly in the side with her elbow. He tried to suppress the gasp of pain, but was unsuccessful.

She winced, looking at him apologetically. He shrugged it off with a forced smile.

"It seems that I am," he said after some time, chuckling slightly at the thought. "Although I cannot decide if that is a good thing or not."

From around the corner, Benja reappeared. His eyes were narrow and his whiskers were twitching with concern.

"Benja! How did it go?" he asked without shouting, knowing that the little creature could hear him clearly even from some distance.

He hurried forward, frowning and shaking his head frantically. Myrddin and Ava's smiles fell to match the expression of the worried mole.

"I am struggling to get a message sent through. The rock here is too dense for the vibrations to travel, and we are too far away from any MoleKind hovels."

Myrddin nodded, storing a tidbit of information away for later use. The homes of the MoleKind were called hovels.

"We need to make haste, but first we must contact the MoleKind in the area as they would know the best place for the people to go to next. Do you know where the next closest hovel is?" he asked.

"I think so." the Benja sniffed. "It would be about a day's journey."

"And with all these injured people?" the prince asked, gesturing at an ancient dwarf warrior whose right leg ended in a stump below the knee.

Benja looked at them as well, rubbing his snout with his hand thoughtfully. "Right. A day and a half then." he paused. "If I can convince the others to take them temporarily, they might also be willing to meet us halfway and help move the sick and injured."

"Excellent idea, Benja. Your wisdom continues to impress me." he said proudly.

The little mole nodded humbly and turned to leave, but then he paused and turned back to face Myrddin. He bowed his head and looked at the ground as he spoke. "I know the opinion of one such as myself would not hold sway at the royal court of the elves..."

At the mention of the Elven court, Myrddin's eyebrow raised.

The little mole continued, still looking down and wringing his hands nervously, "but for what it is worth, I think that you would make a most excellent king. You have the best interest of the people at heart and you always put their needs before your own."

Ava beamed and nodded as she watched the exchange.

Myrddin's quizzical expression melted into a warm smile.

"Thank you Benja," he said, placing his hand on the little creature's shoulder. He paused and waited for the mole to raise his head a meet his gaze before he continued. "It does mean a lot to me, from such a dear MoleKind friend."

The little creature's eyes widened larger than Myrddin had ever seen them before. They were so big that the prince could almost see the vestiges of Benja's original human ancestry peeking through.

"A friend?" the little Mole spluttered out in surprise.

"Of course Benja," the prince said, making sure that his tone conveyed that the idea of thinking anything otherwise might simply be ridiculous, "One of the best."

"Thank you. Thank you, my prince." He looked down again for a moment. When his head rose again, he was twitching with excitement and determination. "I'll go forward and see if I can convince them. It should be easy once I mention your name."

The prince nodded, although he was not nearly as convinced as the other creature. "We will try to get as close as we can. Leave us a trail that the humans and others can follow."

The little creature looked thoughtful for a moment, then his eyes brightened into a knowing grin.

"Alright," he nodded fervently. "See you soon."

He scurried away, and before he faded from sight, Myrddin saw him raise his sharp claws and dig them into the wall, pulling them along behind him as he walked. The mole sliced deep into the stone and made a perfect train of three lines. He had deliberately sliced across a vein of the glowing rock, so it could be seen clearly. Plus, the gashes in the rock were deep enough that even one of the blinded residents could recognize it as they felt their way along the cave walls.

Myrddin shook his head and chuckled to himself as the mole skittered down the tunnel. He turned to see that Cedar and two of the volunteers were returning.

"We think we might have found our next destination, or at least be close to doing so." he said to them cautiously.

The dryad's leafy eyebrows rose into an expression of disbelief, bordering on suspicion.

"So soon? Where are we going?" she asked.

"Benja has gone off to seek the help of the nearest MoleKind hovel," he said, making sure that he used the correct terminology. "They usually keep themselves separate because of the animosity between all the races, but Benja thinks he can convince them to help us. And I am developing a deep respect for his abilities."

"Do you think they will be willing to accept us?" Strondomir spoke up. His voice, though still low and gruff, had lost the belligerent tone of before. In its place was the sound of genuine concern for his party. "Of course we have some MoleKind among our group, but will they welcome..." He looked at Ava, then looked around cautiously. "... even the humans?"

At this, Ava stepped forward. She looked at Strondomir, then at the rest of the group as she spoke.

"Nobody knows better than me how much the rest of the world hates us. And I was none too fond of the little..."

Myrddin's mouth shot open to interrupt whatever derogatory term was about to emerge from Ava's lips, but she caught herself in time. She fidgeted for a second, took a breath, and continued.

"Alright, I hated pretty much everybody. I wear this armor because up there I'd expect to be killed by any one of you. But then I followed Prince Myrddin here, and I saw you people." She stared directly at the blended family of humans and MoleKind as she said this.

The crowd looked around at each other.

"Let's face it. All of our ancestors have probably done horrible things to each other at one point or another. But if we can't get past that, maybe we all deserve to be wiped out by the robots."

Her last sentence reverberated through the cave as the crowd went dead silent.

After a solemn moment, the prince broke the silence. "Benja the MoleKind seemed confident that he could convince the hovel to support you, and I've found him to be a wise and resourceful ally. If they do so, it will be at substantial risk and peril to themselves. If things go well, it could be the beginning of a new era of cooperation and trust among races. But if things go badly..."

He looked around the room as his point sank in.

Cedar stepped forward and continued. "Know that I have set Nolet of the Dryads to lead in my absence, along with Siggebela of the MoleKind, Dostan of the Dwarves, and Jardolin of the Humans. They will lead and protect you as we join Prince Myrddin on his quest. But if the MoleKind hovel will receive us, then we will be their guests and submit to their leadership. Is that understood?"

Some of the crowd nodded enthusiastically. Others less so.

"Very well . We will move as far as we can in the next few hours before resting. I understand you are tired, but we cannot risk staying here. Assist everyone that you can so that we can move as quickly as possible."

The crowd dispersed into several clumps. Ava slipped closer to Myrddin and nodded toward the party that had agreed to join them and fight.

"Some of them are going to be a problem," she whispered.

Droran looked up to see who she was looking at and nodded his head in agreement. "They have never had a taste of power before."

"I know," Myrddin said simply, a tired sigh escaping him. "I can already tell we have a few troublemakers, but we are stuck with them. Hopefully, having an outside enemy to fight will give us enough unity to function."

"You think we will see battle soon?" Droran asked. His tone was much too eager for the prince's liking.

"I expect we will. Probably sooner than we like." he confirmed under Ava's thoughtful gaze. "The robot and the drone army have to be stopped and the longer we wait, the larger they grow and the more resources they consume."

"Well," she said, as he prepared himself mentally for her to bid him good luck and turn around to go home, "I suppose that somebody has got to do it, so it might as well be us."

He was so relieved that he burst out in a chortle. As he looked to his the little dwarf was nodding furiously.

"I think if it isn't us," he stated solemnly, "it will be no one. And that's the problem."

"I didn't sign up for any of this, you know," she said, staring at him with hard eyes. "I just saw that you were in trouble in the fight and decided that you needed some help. Now I am here, thousands of leagues underground, stuck in some grand adventure to save the world."

He met her stare, speaking gently, but directly. "You can leave at any point, Ava. You certainly don't owe me anything. If you like, you can even join the refugees. They need someone to look out for them. I would certainly think no less of you."

They stood for several long seconds, searching each other's eyes. At first, they both looked like they were about to say something more. Then, they fell into a wordless conversation that neither seemed to be eager to interrupt until the buzz of activity in the room grew to the point it shook them out of the moment.

Ava broke away with an awkward laugh.

"Nice try, but you're not getting rid of me that easy. I'm much more comfortable in a battle up topside than down here babysitting."

Myrddin matched the turn of her mood. "Well, I am glad that I could help you." he said, smiling.

They walked through the crowds and helped a few refugees shoulder their burdens until everyone was ready to go.

Myrddin grasped his sword, which was still stuck in the ground. He uttered an Elvish phrase and pulled it up. As he did, the sword and the veins of mineral dimmed.

"Cedar and I will take the lead and Ava will take the rear. Other leaders spread yourselves through the group. Help us keep up the pace and report any problems."

And with that, the ragged community was underway. Progress was slow. In the darker tunnels, Myrddin would lead, holding his sword aloft for light. As they reached tunnels with plenty of lighted mineral, Myrddin would instruct Cedar to take point, and he would filter through the crowd to see how the people were faring.

Overall, he was pleased with how well this beleaguered community had bonded, even with the addition of himself and his party. But he still saw restlessness among several of the dwarves, and there was a tension among the dryads that was hard to discern.

Then there was Droran, who was a sparkling bundle of energy. Too much energy for many of those around him. He wove in and out of the crowd, offering to help and speaking words of hope and encouragement. Sometimes, the help was welcome, but most people were too tired to endure his constant talking.

Visiting with the people encouraged him, but each time he returned to the front, he found that Cedar had picked up her pace to the point where the slower members of the group weren't able to keep up. Rather than risking an open confrontation with the dryad, he would resume his position at the front, and stand still until everyone had caught up, much to Cedar's annoyance. After hours of this cycle had passed, they came to a large, open cavern, and he held up his hand.

"We'll stop here for now," he said, feeling Cedar's glare on him immediately. "We'll need to keep moving again, so it will only be for a short while. Those of you who can, get some sleep. I need a few volunteers to keep watch with me."

He rubbed his hands across his face and looked around to receive the volunteers that would keep watch with him. But none appeared, other than Ava and Droran. Cedar folded her arms and retired to a corner of the cave. The others either sat gratefully or simply collapsed.

He sighed as he reached into his travel bag and pulled out what was left of his water skin. The once round and bulging skin was now thin. He started to pull it to his lips, then he looked around the room. He walked over to Cedar, who was still sulking in the corner. Myrddin passed the skin to the dryad, whispering to her to give it to those who needed it the most.

The look of scorn in her eyes softened. Water was necessary to any breathing creature, but to a dryad, it was sacred. He nodded to her, and she bowed her head as she received the skin from his hands.

As she walked into the crowd, Droran jumped up from where he had sat only a moment before and greeted the prince. "Well, that's enough rest for me!" he said with a grin. "Sentry Droran ready for service, my prince! Where shall I stand guard?"

Myrddin laughed and shook his head.

"Thank you, Droran," he said. "Why don't you stand over there at the exit to the cave? Make sure nothing comes in so the people can rest."

"Aye, my prince!" The dwarf bowed and thumped his fist on his chest, then marched toward the tunnel entrance like a soldier in a dress parade.

"You should get some sleep too," Ava's voice intruded suddenly, as she approached the prince. "By my reckoning, we've been driving the people for almost two days, and the two days it took us to get to Last Chance weren't exactly a vacation either."

Myrddin rubbed his eyes and blinked wide. The dim green light from the cave walls made the dark circles under his eyes look even darker. Contrasting with his pale elven skin and hair, he looked ghoulish.

Had it really been so long since he had woken up in Ava's home? It felt like it had only been a day or so ago. But his life in the royal courts of the elves seemed like a distant memory, even though he had only been gone from of the Elven kingdom for a week or so. He had experienced so much already, but his father might not have noticed he was missing. Evakhan might still have been carrying out all of his responsibilities for him without having been caught.

He shook off his thoughts and stared intently at Ava. Her eye bags were less prominent, but there were definitely there. And her eyes were red from squinting in the dim light.

"It's been the same amount of time for you," he said to Ava, who replied by frowning and crossing her arms over her chest plate.

"No really, I'll be fine," he assured her after seeing her frown. "I am better suited to it. I will rest once we reach the MoleKind and the people are safe, or at least... safer. You get some rest, and I will go back to the rear and guard the entrance. We'll have to leave again in a few hours, and you'll need to be sharp."

Ava rolled her eyes. "Alright. As long as you promise to get some rest once we find the hovel."

"Agreed."

Ava pulled her hair out of its tight ponytail and let it flow over her shoulders. She laid her helmet on the cave floor and curled up, using the helmet as a pillow. The prince watched as she fell asleep almost instantly.

In the pale light, even in armor, with sweat and dirt on her cheeks, she was a beauty. He allowed himself the luxury of letting his mind wander. She was so fierce, and yet so caring. She would make a glorious queen.

As the implications of his daydream sank in, he shuddered and shook himself back into reality. A human woman? And queen of what? His, and all the other "kingdoms" were dead or dying. He took one more look at the sleeping warrior in her robot armor and slipped quietly to the back of the group.

His bones felt heavy with exhaustion, and he was struggling to keep his eyes open.

He sat in the back of the cave and observed the refugees. Some were sleeping heavily, but some were too badly injured or in pain to sleep. A few parents woke from time to time and checked on their children.

He reached out with his magic occasionally, sending tendrils out in every direction, almost as if he were creating a bubble around them, trying to make sure that they were still alone. Each attempt was more difficult than the last. His range was decreasing rapidly, and he could barely maintain his focus for more than a few seconds. Finally, he gave up, realizing if he closed his eyes one more time to focus within, he would probably fall asleep.

He rose and slipped forward to check on Droran, passing a sleeping Ava on the way.

"Anything to report, sentry Droran?" Myrddin said with a smile.

"No, my prince. It's been as quiet as a tomb."

The prince's nose wrinkled at the description and the dwarf caught himself.

"I'm sorry, that was probably not the best way to say that. I mean to say, um, everything is fine."

"Very well, my friend. It's time to wake the people."

"Aye, my prince!" The dwarf shouted excitedly. Nearby, Ava moaned and rolled over at the sudden noise. Droran put a hand up to his mouth to yell a wakeup call, but Myrddin grabbed them and pulled them down.

"Droran!" The prince whispered. "Wake them quietly. One at a time."

"Aye! Sorry." The dwarf whispered and nodded as he scurried into the crowd.

Chapter 12

They trudged along for another day. Myrddin drove the weary group as far as possible between rest breaks, but the breaks were getting closer and closer together as the journey took its toll on the crowd. Most of the refugees shuffled forward, mindlessly putting one foot in front of the other like a march of the undead. Droran's seemingly boundless enthusiasm was finding its bounds. Cedar's impatience was returning.

"We can't keep this up much longer." Ava whispered to Myrddin during the third break. Or was it the fourth? Myrddin's tired mind was having trouble keeping up.

"I know. But what choice do we have?" He replied solemnly.

"I insist you rest this time, Myrddin!" she whispered in a tone which sounded more like a shout. "I've gotten to sleep several times now. You're losing your edge. Now I'm standing guard and you're resting. Prince or no prince, I'm giving you an order!"

"Fair enough." He sighed. "The last thing I have energy for is to argue with you." Myrddin shook his head, leaned back against the cavern wall, and slid his body down into a seated position. He crossed his legs and put his palms over his eyes. Just as he began to doze, his inner sense jolted him awake again. He felt a forceful presence moving through the tunnels rapidly.

When he reached out with his magic, he detected an enormous creature, or rather a considerable group of creatures, dashing through the tunnels; they seemed to glow with a rich brown light, each individual differing slightly in shade and brightness.

Their magical signatures seemed familiar to him, but he could not recognize their race or form. He tried to track them, but they were fairly far away. As he felt through the veins of enchanted rock, he also discerned that this group was in a group of tunnels which was not directly connected to the tunnel they were in. He decided they must just be a group of scurrying animals, and that since they couldn't reach their cave, they wouldn't be a threat.

Having decided they were safe again, he bowed his head again to rest. But within seconds he was awakened by an even stronger sensation of impending life and movement.

When he reached out with his magic again, he sensed that this unknown presence, was much closer than they had been before. He also noticed they had moved to a place which had been solid stone moments before.

"What is going on?" he whispered quietly to himself. He dragged himself to to stand and placed his hand on the hilt of his sword.

Ava and Droran were close enough to overhear him and to see him rise. The dwarf looked confused. Ava recognized his stance and the look on his face. She instantly stepped in front of the large group, placing her helmet on her head and drawing her weapons as she looked carefully into the dark tunnel.

Myrddin did the same, drawing his enchanted sword from the ground and moving to stand next to her.

He checked yet again, reaching out with his magic. He did not have to go far at all this time, and his findings only confirmed what he had thought was happening before. The large group of creatures was moving through the rock, creating a new tunnel which was bringing them directly toward the straggling refugees.

The prince prepared his sword as they closed in. Gripping it as tightly as his damaged hand allowed but pointing it away from where the threat was about to appear.

"Don't get ahead of yourself," he said to both Ava and the rambunctious Droran who were both in full battle stance, weapons raised and ready.

There was a faint rumbling and scraping noise, which got louder and louder by the minute, waking most of the refugees. Several of the volunteer warriors stood behind the prince, who held up his free hand, cautioning the others not to take any action without his command.

Moments later, the wall of the tunnel in front of them caved inwards, creating a cloud of dust and smoke. They all stepped back, covering their mouths and coughing. They backed up a safe distance and formed what might become a defensive line if necessary.

As the smoke cleared, they were presented with a curious sight.

A stocky, rotund MoleKind appeared, much larger than Benja. And then another one, and another. Soon, a dozen or more MoleKind had filed into the little tunnel.

While Myrddin and his party looked shocked, the attitude of the MoleKind troop was disarmingly nonchalant. Clearly, burrowing through rock and breaking an entrance into a new tunnel was a daily occurrence to them. They cocked their heads curiously at the elf and dwarf with swords drawn, and the strange robot standing beside them.

Myrddin studied the troop of moles. Having only met Benja, he had assumed they probably all had his same red eyes and brown fur. That assumption was completely incorrect. He was amazed at the variety of their shapes, sizes, and colors. Some of them were nearly as tall as an elf, others even tinier than Benja. Their fur colors included dark brown, gray, reddish, and some with hair almost as pale as his own. Their eyes were red, or brown, or green, or as blue as his own.

It dawned on him, of course, they were descended from humans. Naturally, they would have a similar variety of shapes and sizes to their ancestor race.

One of the human 'soldiers' who had sworn himself to Myrddin's leadership only a few hours before pushed past the prince, pointing a small knife at the nearest MoleKind, an immense creature with golden fur, bright green eyes, and unusually straight teeth. "What's your business here?" the man sneered.

Before the elf prince could pull him back, the giant mole swatted the man with a backhanded swipe of his claw. The blow, from a claw which was made to dig through solid rock, sent the man flying against the cave wall. As it was a backhanded blow, the scratches on the man's body from the claws' sharp tips were only superficial.

Myrddin reasoned that if it had been a front-handed swipe, the human's body would have been shredded into a stack of clean slices, like a game bird on a platter. The human would have been dead before he realized what happened.

The man's pitiful knife fell from his hands as his back hit the wall and he slumped to the ground. Cedar the dryad vaulted over to him and kicked the knife in the opposite direction of the moles. As it clattered away down the tunnel, she drew him to his feet by the neck and raised her hand to strike him.

"Stop!" cried the prince. "Everyone calm down!"

Cedar lowered her striking hand but kept her grasp on his throat. She tightened her grip slightly and glared at him threateningly. He bowed his head as she led him away, chastising him all the while.

Even from a distance, Myrddin could hear her whispered shouts at the man. "Fool! How dare you defy a direct order from the prince? What were you thinking? In the first place, they didn't attack. In the second place, he was bigger than you! And such a silly little knife..." Her thinly hushed insults trailed off down the tunnel in the direction they had entered.

Myrddin was almost glad Cedar had finally found a target for the pent-up anger she'd been carrying.

The next thought which ran through the prince's mind was another surprising revelation about the MoleKind as a race. Because of Benja's tiny frame and diplomatic nature, he was expecting a race of meek, and for the lack of a better description, mousy beings. The sharp claws and powerful arms of the mole standing before him showed him they were powerful creatures who were not to be trifled with.

He also realized just how much damage the mole COULD have done to his would-be attacker if he had chosen to, and how much restraint he had shown. That told him all he needed to know.

He sheathed his sword and stepped forward, waving to Ava to remove her helmet. He raised his hand in greeting to the MoleKind who had been assaulted.

"My sincerest apologies," he said, bowing his head slightly, "please forgive the man. His attitude does not represent our group. We mean no harm."

The MoleKind in front of him smiled warmly and waved his paw nonchalantly.

"Do not worry, Prince Myrddin of the Elves," he beamed. "Times are dangerous, and I suppose our entrance was a bit of a surprise. His reaction is understandable."

"Nevertheless," Myrddin continued, "your forgiveness is gracious, and I thank you for it."

The MoleKind nodded his head.

"Might I ask your name?" Myrddin said. "As you are clearly aware of mine."

"Of course," laughed the giant mole. His voice was deep and booming, another stark contrast from Benja. "My name is Brock, and I am from the mole hovel nearest to here. Your friend, Benja, has told us you need our help, and we have come personally to welcome you into our home and to assist you in your travels. The tunnel we've just created will lead you directly there, taking many days off of your journey. We've also brought some fresh food, water, and healing supplies to strengthen your people for this last leg of their trip."

Myrddin and Ava stared at Brock, then at each other with wide eyes.

The prince nodded toward the people, and Brock waved his massive paw at the moles behind him. They proceeded to move amongst the refugees, dispensing supplies and giving what medical care they could.

"Thank you for your great kindness, Brock of the MoleKind," the prince said. "These people would not have been able to survive for much longer without your help."

"It is our pleasure, Prince Myrddin." he chimed. "We do not often have guests, and hospitality toward the needy is an important part of our culture."

He pondered the concept of "MoleKind Culture." Those two words together had an odd ring in his Elven ears. "Where is Benja?" he asked absentmindedly.

"Right over here," he heard a voice calling from the back of the MoleKind pack.

He spun around to see his little friend, whom he now understood was one of the smaller members of his race. So small, he had been hidden behind the more robust members of his party. But his hearing was still keen, as he must have heard Myrddin asking after him from the back of the pack.

"Thank you, again my friend." He said, bowing his head even lower than Benja's, which was a long stretch for the gangly elf. "You are quite the diplomat and tactician. I hope someday to introduce you to my friend Bayard. The two of you have much in common."

For about an hour, the MoleKind moved among the refugees, preparing them for the journey. Even Myrddin received some porridge of root vegetables, which he found to be surprisingly flavorful.

While Brock and the others attended to their duties, Ava approached the prince.

"So, what do you think about our new hosts? Can we trust them?" she whispered with almost no breath in her voice, aware of the sensitive ears of the moles.

Myrddin replied in kind. "I think if they had any intention other than to help us, we'd all be dead already."

She replied with a shrug.

Chapter 13

At last, Myrddin and Brock agreed that the group was as ready as they were going to be, and they set off down the tunnel the moles had created. Brock, Myrddin, and two of the larger moles lead the way. They seemed to have deliberately tunneled through areas with well-lit minerals, so Myrddin was able to keep his sword in its sheath.

Ava returned to her rear position along with several of the moles, who also had the bearing of warriors. Within a few minutes, the human woman and the stocky moles were swapping stories of battles with robots and encounters with arachnids.

Finally, the group came upon a gigantic pile of stones which looked like they had fallen there naturally and appeared to block their path going forward. The prince frowned and looked around, wondering how this could have happened in the short time since the moles had tunnelled their way to meet him.

Brock saw the prince's expression. He had been waiting for it. His snout broke into a huge toothy grin as he reached into the pile and pulled a single, hidden lever, causing the entire structure to swing up like a drawbridge.

He beamed mightily and extended his arm with a bow. "Welcome to our hovel, Prince Myrddin of the elves! We do not name our hovels, but this one is our home and you and your people are honored guests."

Myrddin was raised in the royal court and had been taught how to keep back his emotions, especially surprise. But as he entered the MoleKind hovel, he could not stop his eyes from growing wide and his mouth from gaping open.

He had been expecting to see a room made of stone and dirt, with maybe a few rooms leading off from them, also made of stone and dirt. But he realized, hopefully once and for all, he had been thinking too much of the moles, as animals, forgetting the human heritage that the MoleKind had come from.

To his amazement, they had created an underground city. And a beautiful one at that. It had the ingenuity of the dwarven caves, but with an elegance and artistic quality which reminded him of elven villages.

It was made of one enormous cavern, with dozens of attractive homes carved into stone walls of the cavern. Each had a set of stairs, a painted door of thatched vines, and a balcony which overlooked the central area. Many balconies were decorated with paintings and sculptures, and each was painted in various colors, with rich red seeming to be the most popular, but yellow, blue, and white homes also lined the sides of the cave. Many of the homes had veins of the glowing mineral flowing through them, and the MoleKind residents had chosen pigment colors to complement the lights in a way that brought a wide smile to Myrddin's tired face.

The hidden door through which they entered was at the top of a slope, about three quarters of the way up the cavern wall. From that vantage point, he could see streets which had been carefully cobbled with octagonal stones laid in a decorative pattern. They were worn down from what appeared to be decades, or even centuries, of travel. Upon the streets were MoleKind of all shapes, sizes, and colors; some walking, some clumped in conversation, and some pulling wooden carts laden with vegetables and clay jugs.

In the center of the town, or hovel as he reminded himself, Myrddin saw a building which was much larger than the others. Its shape was more angular than the smooth curves of the homes and shops. Having grown up as a prince, he recognized a place of government when he saw one. He searched his memory, but his Elven tutors had taught him nothing about how the MoleKind leadership functioned.

"What is the building in the center?" he asked Benja quietly.

"It's our town hall." the little creature replied matter-of-factly. "Where we go to settle a disagreement or to get permission to do anything in the hovel which might affect the community. You'll see. It's where we're going now."

"We are going to meet with the rulers of the hovel?" asked Myrddin.

Benja shook his head and snorted before pointing to Brock. "You already have! We are just going there because it's where the extra food and medical supplies are stored."

Myrddin nodded slowly. His appreciation of this race and their culture was growing by the minute.

As they walked along the houses and shops which lined the main street, Myrddin could not help but notice all of their eyes were upon him and the refugees who followed. Those gathered in conversation stopped and stared. Furry children tugged at their parents' arms and pointed their long fingers at the newcomers.

But what surprised, and encouraged him, was the fact that the MoleKind did not seem to be threatened or upset by their presence. Even when they gasped at Ava in her robot armor, their expressions did not portray the hatred and prejudice he had seen and been taught to expect from anyone outside his own people. He saw curiosity, or perhaps wonder, in their faces, but not the least bit of malice.

"I've told them we won't be staying long," Benja said. "They would have kept us for a few days otherwise, or permanently, if they could. It is our way to welcome those in need, but to welcome a Prince of the Elves, well, that's something else altogether."

Myrddin nodded, thankful for Benja's insight. For once, his royal identity gave him a feeling of warmth, rather than regret.

Looking to his side, he noticed Ava's face was taut with concentration. Her gaze swiveled back and forth in a military surveillance of the area. Her gait was stiff, and she kept hands close to her helmet and her weapon.

When they reached the base of the larger building, Myrddin was surprised to find that it was far more ornate than he had perceived from a distance.

It was made from stone, but it was far from rough. Instead, there were elegant carvings on every available surface. Myrddin peered closely at a stone column and ran his fingers over a depiction of three MoleKind warriors fighting an enormous arachnid. The intricacy of the carvings astounded him, but then it occurred to him... these people carved rock with their fingernails. Carving on stone for them would be like doodling on parchment for an elf.

By briefly scanning the images on the way into the building, Myrddin learned more about the MoleKind than any elf had known. The icons illustrated every aspect of their history and of their current daily lives. He could see how they gathered and prepared food, how they worked and played, how they fought and buried their dead. A historical wall displayed scenes which chronicled the building on this hovel, back through the Great Change, and all the way back to the time of their human ancestry.

The prince wished he wasn't in such a hurry to get on with his mission and meet with the centaurs. He would have enjoyed staying here for weeks and learning more about this fascinating race and their ways.

They entered the building to find a host of MoleKind in waiting to greet them. Some dressed in white coats and caps, the garb of human medical and scientific professionals from before the change, while others wore brown aprons and smelled faintly of herbs and stew. Most of them were more plump than their comrades, probably the cooks.

"We are honored to have prince Myrddin of the elves, and the citizens of Last Chance in our presence," the golden-haired MoleKind said again.

He stood in the building's doorway and spoke outward so the gathering crowd could hear him.

"Although the prince himself cannot stay long, we are honored that he has selected us to be the start of a new era, where MoleKind, humans, dwarves, dryads, elves and all other races will prove we can work together and live in harmony. We will introduce them into the society soon, but first they must rest," and with that, Brock turned back inside.

Cheers of approval from outside drifted in on the breeze, and the prince was glad to hear the population seemed to be happy.

Brock explained order of activities for getting the refugees settled. There would be different rooms for cleaning, eating, and having medical needs seen to. There would also be rooms with beds where people could rest and recuperate.

"This is quite a city, my apologies, hovel, you have here, Brock." The prince shared in admiration.

"The architecture, artwork, and the kindness of your people is overwhelming."

"Our people went through turbulent times in the days just after the Great Change." Brock explained. "There were battles and trials as we learned to deal with the reality of our new form. Many hated what we were turning into and longed for the days of being 'truly human'. But over the years, we've learned to embrace our lives and our new abilities. But to be honest, I'm thankful to you, Prince Myrddin."

"How so?" the prince asked.

"First, you're giving our people something fresh to do, and to learn. Second, while we've carved out a pleasant life in the caverns, we know it's only a matter of time until the machines break into our world as well."

The prince nodded as Cedar approached, with the ragged squad of volunteers hanging just outside the entrance behind her.

"Now that the refugees are settled, we want to know how soon we can leave." She stated.

Myrddin looked back over her shoulder at the group, wondering again if he had made the right choice in accepting their offer. "Tell those who are joining us." he whispered. "They should eat and rest here and meet us outside the centaur forest in three days."

"But we are ready to follow you now." the dryad insisted.

"And follow my into battle you shall." the prince assured her. "But the centaurs are powerful and mercurial, and they have only called me. They may welcome me alone, or with a companion, but if I enter their lands with an armed party, they might take it as an offence. Use this time to train and organize them as best you can. See if the moles can help with training and equipment."

Cedar's leafy eyebrows narrowed. She crossed her arms across her chest. "Very well. I will do my best to keep them occupied." She strutted off as Ava, who had been sitting in an adjacent room with one of the nurses, approached.

"That didn't look like fun." She quipped, shaking her head.

"I'm still not sure if they'll do us harm or good, but it would be no use having them slaughtered by the centaurs before we even see battle with the machines."

"So, when do we leave?" she asked.

"We will rest tonight and leave first thing in the morning," he replied.

"Works for me." she said, and headed toward the sleeping quarters.

Myrddin walked into the makeshift cafeteria the MoleKind had set up in a meeting room. The rest of his part had already eaten, and the moles were cleaning up the place settings. He slouched into a chair at the end of a long table and one of the plump, apron-wearing moles brought him a steaming bowl of stew, a whole loaf of warm crusty bread, and a jug of berry wine. It was a simple meal, but after his adventures of the last few days, it seemed like a feast.

He tried to savor the meal, and he didn't want to overfill himself to the point of feeling sluggish, but the smells and flavors overcame him and he inhaled his dinner in a matter of seconds. His MoleKind attendant giggled at the sight of the noble prince with wine and stew dripping from the sides of his mouth. She scurried off and returned immediately, handing him a towel and another, larger, serving.

Once Myrddin had eaten his fill, an assistant appeared and escorted him to the healing station, where His wounds were inspected and tended to by the nurse. Upon inspecting them, she frowned and said, "Wait here just a moment, please". She left the room.

Myrddin's eyes narrowed. He was well versed in healing, and was not fearful, but it was never good when a healer looked at you with such an expression. He looked around the room, fidgeting.

After a short time, the nurse came back into the room with three leather pouches. She emptied their contents onto the table at his side. His eyes widened and his mouth drew into a broad smile. She looked up at him with understanding and smiled back at him.

"These... these are the very herbs I need to complete my healing!" he exclaimed. "How did you know?"

"We have many ways of collecting information and have been doing so for centuries. I know little about Elven magical healing, but we often use a combination of these herbs for wounds like yours. I thought they might be helpful." She said proudly.

The nurse helped him prepare the herbs, and then watched him as he applied them and performed his healing incantation. She watched in wonder as his skin slowly regained its form and color.

"I would still like to wrap your side with bandages for protection." She said.

The prince nodded.

"Thank you," he said to the little MoleKind as she finished trying the fresh bandages, giving them a tug to make sure they would not come undone.

"It's a pleasure," she said, followed swiftly by, "You really should be more careful though."

The prince laughed, which brought a smile to the little MoleKind's face as well. "I'll do my best, but I'm afraid I can't promise anything," he said.

She chuckled at him, cuffing his ear slightly, before waving him off and moving on to the next person on her list.

The prince wandered down the hallway to the room they had prepared for him. The warmth of the food and wine relaxed him, and for the first time in days, he was not in pain. He continued to marvel at the carvings and paintings that decorated the halls of the building. One painting just outside his room caught his eye. It was a large MoleKind sitting on a throne, surrounded by smaller moles, presumably his family.

Myrddin thought of his own father, King of the proud Elven race, now holed up in a dark, smelly closet. And yet here was a race which most others looked down upon, which was thriving both in culture and in kindness to strangers. He let out a long sigh and entered his room.

He washed himself in the basin of water which had been provided for him. Instead of putting on his old tunic, or rather the few scraps that remained of it, he opted to put on the spare he had brought along. It was his last one, but he'd hopefully be visiting the seer of the centaurs and he wanted to look presentable.

He laid back into the soft little pillow and pulled the coarse blanket up to his chin. Within a few moments, he had drifted off. Almost three days without sleep, combined with all the activity and injury which had occurred in those three days, finally caught up to him, and he was out like a candle before another thought could flit through his mind.

He regained consciousness to the feeling of something, or rather someone, tapping against his face.

He struggled for a few moments to open his sleep-encrusted eyes before he could make out the face of a beautiful angel above him. He was just about to call out to her and ask her if he had died when the angel spoke.

"You've slept for almost ten hours. We need to get going soon or we'll lose what's left of the lead we have on the robots." the rude angel said.

Wait. Rude angel? He sat up rapidly, rubbing his eyes as he realized what Ava had said.

"Ten hours! Why did you let me sleep for so long?" he complained in a groggy voice.

Her mouth slid into a grin.

"That is an interesting hairstyle. But seriously, we should get going." she taunted as she slipped out of the room.

He sighed tiredly before slipping his boots onto his feet, slipping his travel bag onto his shoulder and walking outside. He found his three companions - Droran, Ava and Benja - all waiting for him, ready to depart.

They nodded to one another, starting on their journey without another word.

Chapter 14

Benja led them from the town hall building through the streets of the hovel. It was early by their timekeeping and few people were out. The passersby did not speak, but all nodded warmly as they passed.

They moved briskly, without conversation. Benja led the way. From time to time, he would burrow a shortcut tunnel to speed their journey. Myrddin used those times to reach out with his magic to look for threats. Ava was ever vigilant and for once, Droran focused his energy on the journey and didn't distract the others with questions. He simply hummed a dwarven battle ballad quietly to himself.

Their teamwork helped them avoid arachnids and other distractions. With Benja connecting the extensive tunnels for them, they made quick work. They were consistently sloping upward, but the rest and food had rejuvenated them, and the upward path didn't slow them down.

Eventually, they came to a cave whose walls appeared darker than the rest, and whose ceiling was relatively low, a little less than twice the height of Myrddin.

"It looks like this is it. I can smell the wetter consistency of the soil," Benja said, his little snout wriggling. "The next leg of our journey is in that direction." He said, pointing straight up.

"And just how is that supposed to work?" Ava asked. "We aren't exactly built for climbing vertical walls."

"I don't know yet," the little creature replied, "but there's always a way. I'll help as best I can."

He glanced at Myrddin as if asking for permission to go forward, which the elf gave with a nod of his head.

The rest of the party stood back as the little MoleKind climbed up the wall until he was hanging from the ceiling. Then, using one arm to keep himself anchored, he dug with the other. In moments, a rather impressive hole appeared. Those on the ground stepped back as piles of dirt and dust began to fall.

Fortunately, Benja had been correct, and the ground here was saturated with water. Soon the parched soil mixed with stone was replaced by dark dirt, coming down in torrents as the little mole disappeared into the hole to continue its digging.

The top of Benja's body disappeared into the hole, leaving his feet and tail hanging out. For a second, there was a scramble as if he had lost his grip, and the party below shifted in confusion, wondering whether to get out of the way or to try to catch him when he fell.

But he regained his grip and the tiny feet shot up into the hole and braced themselves against the wall of the tunnel. There was a momentary pause and then his whole body disappeared into the hole, and a cascade of soil poured out of the hole at astounding speed.

This continued for a few more moments, until suddenly, the soil was replaced by a ray of sunlight as the digging stopped.

Stepping forward, almost wary of the ray, Myrddin paused for a moment before allowing it to wash over him. It warmed his skin in ways that he could barely remember in the back of his mind, and he was let out a satisfied smile, feeling more refreshed than he had felt in a while. He had not realized how much he had missed the sun.

Looking up, he saw the long tunnel, opening up to reveal a myriad of greenery, as well as small patches of blue and white where the sky above was visible. It was so open that he experienced a sensation akin to vertigo. His magic-enhanced senses had adapted to the underground environment much like his eyes had, and his entire being swooned as it adjusted to the open world above, whose presence was now pouring into his senses.

His view of the sky was disrupted by the head of a very proud-looking MoleKind.

"Benja," he called up the hole. "You've done it!"

The little creature's chuckle echoed into the tunnel. Myrddin could only smile .

"That's wonderful, but now how do we get up there?" Ava inquired.

He tried to estimate the distance between the top and the bottom of the little hole. If he raised his hands, he would barely be able to touch the ceiling and the hole along with it. After that, it was probably another two of his lengths until they would breach the surface.

Ava and Droran also gathered around him in the sunlight as they tried to think of some way to get the rest of them up. Benja slowly made his way back down to them, inserting his sharp claws into the firm surface to climb effortlessly. He reached the bottom of the hole and hung upside down, gripping the inside of the hole with his feet. He crossed his arms nonchalantly, as if this inverted pose was a commonplace way to converse.

Given the height of the cave, the upside-down mole's face was almost at the same height as the elf, and Ava suppressed a giggle at the absurdity of the scene.

"I don't suppose that you'd be able to lift one of us there?" Droran asked, his voice indicating he already knew what the answer would be.

"Actually," Benja said as he searched around, scratching his head before changing his mind, "probably not."

The group smiled and shrugged. As they did so, a bit of tree root dislodged from the hole and plunked right on Droran's head. "Hey now!" He shouted.

"Wait, what sort of vegetation is up there?" Ava asked the mole. "Are they more fern-like trees or do they have vines?"

The little creature shook his head, seemingly already knowing why the human was asking. "There aren't any trees with vines yet. Maybe a little bit deeper into the forest, but I'm reluctant to travel that way on my own.

Myrddin nodded. Not only was this the surface world, which Benja had never been to, but it was also the forest that the centaurs inhabited. Even if this was not strictly centaur territory yet, they might run into one.

"What about roots?" she asked again, glancing at the tunnel again. "Is there anything up there long enough for us to climb with?"

"Let me check," the little creature said. "I might find something."

He went up again, leaving them at the bottom. After a few minutes, the group got concerned. Myrddin tried to lift Droran on his shoulders, which allowed him to reach the hole, but the ground was too slick for the dwarf to gain traction with his hands, and he fell back to the ground.

Finally, Benja returned. He did not have a single root, but instead had a collection of strong, thick roots that he had woven together. He tested every joint where he had carefully knotted them, probably far more than necessary, as he slowly lowered it down into the tunnel. It was just long enough to reach Myrddin's shoulders.

"I'll go first," Ava said. "I'm the lightest so I'll would have the best chance of making it. At least Benja won't have to be alone out there."

Both Myrddin and Droran nodded in agreement.

"Need a hand?" Myrddin asked as she tried to grab hold of the 'rope'. She could barely reach it with her fingers if she stood on her toes and wasn't able to grab it on her own.

"Thank you," she nodded.

He quickly wrapped his arms around her waist and lifted her as high as she would go. It was more than enough, and she wrapped both her arms around the rope, and then her feet as well after she had scrunched her body up.

The elf and dwarf at the bottom waited anxiously, ready to catch her if the roots snapped or she lost her grip. Benja was hanging over the edge at the top too, his feet dug into the ground and his hands outstretched to grab her the moment that she came close enough.

After a bit of grunting and scrambling, Myrddin saw her feet disappear into the sunlight, and her smiling face reappear a second later. She gave Myrddin a "thumbs up" sign.

"Right," Droran said, once she had gotten over successfully, "I suppose I'm next. Care to give me a hand too?"

Myrddin nodded.

While the dwarf was fully a head shorter than Ava, he was much heavier. After having lifted him a few minutes ago, and then lifting Ava, he was feeling strained. His arms started shaking when he stretched them up as far as possible, pushing the stocky dwarf's thighs upward. The dwarf quickly grabbed hold of the roots and Myrddin felt the weight release and Droran scrambled up into the hole.

They all froze as a loud groan came from the roots, protesting against the dwarf's weight. Droran held on, trying to stay perfectly still, and when nothing further happened, he continued upwards. He let out a little yelp of relief when he reached the top, one arm grabbed by the MoleKind and the other by the human to try and get his weight off the roots as quickly as possible.

Now, only the Elven prince remained.

He was probably the heaviest of them all, although only slightly heavier than the dwarf probably, and he would have no one to help him with the first section. He also had his hands to worry about. They had almost completely healed with the help of the MoleKind nurse's herbs, but they were still tender.

Taking a deep breath, he reached up and grabbed onto the roots.

The first section was a struggle, as he was unable to use his legs, and they swung around like dead weight. He took a breath and heaved upward with his arms, making a little more headway. He dug one hand deeply into the weave of the vines and got a firm grip. This allowed him to get his knees wrapped around the bottom of the vines.

As soon as he wrapped his legs around the roots, things started going a little quicker. He was just about to reach the outstretched arms of his friends when another groan echoed through the roots.

He froze, much as Droran had. Turning his head slowly, searched for the origin of the groan. The problem was at the entrance of the hole, where the root was pressed firmly against a sharp piece of rock that was slowly cutting into the root under the pressure of his weight.

He took a deep breath to relax himself and gingerly resumed his climb, keeping his eye on the cut the entire time, watching as it grew. "I may need some help here." He called. Droran and Ava both leaned into the hole to assist.

As Myrddin neared the top of the hole, he grabbed the dwarf's hand just as the rope snapped. Ava grabbed his other hand and they yanked as hard as they could.

The root rope slithered down the hole like a retreating serpent and crashed to the bottom of the cave. His hands, which had been almost completely healed a while ago, were now torn and in tremendous pain again.

They all fell onto the damp grass, panting in the sunlight.

It was the dwarf that started laughing first, reminding Myrddin of when they had made it through the gates at Last Chance. He gladly joined in as before, the adrenaline pumping through his veins combined with the blue sky and trees above them, making him feel absolutely giddy.

They laid there for some time, simply breathing in the fresh air and appreciating their modest victory.

He heard Ava next to him, inhaling deeply. "I never thought that I would smell fresh air again," she said.

He hummed in agreement as he breathed it in. He could taste the dew in the back of his throat, and the nectar from some flowers that must have been nearby. "So sweet..." he mumbled.

Finally, when their breathing had gone back to normal, he sat up, gazing over his friends. They opened their eyes and smiled back at him except for Benja, whose eyes were squeezed his eyes tightly shut and covered with one paw while he acclimated to the bright sunlight.

"Well done, everyone," he said with a smile on his face. "We have made it to the surface. And now we get to go meet the centaurs."

Ava groaned next to him, while Droran's face burst into a smile.

"I can't believe we still have to do that. Can't we just stay here for a while and pretend we have nothing else to do?" Ava mumbled, her hands on her face muffling the sound of her grumbling.

"Oh, come now!" Droran laughed at her, tapping her lightly on the side. "Adventure awaits us!"

Myrddin could not quite make out her mumbling, but he was sure that he caught something about 'crazy dwarf' and 'self-preservation'. He imagined he probably would have agreed with her.

Myrddin kneeled next to Benja, who still had his eyes firmly shut.

"You did it, my friend. Thank you."

Benja slowly cracked open his eyes and smiled, "It's no wonder you lot were squinting down there all the time, didn't your parents ever tell you if you gazed into the light you'd go blind? It's all light up here!"

Myrddin laughed.

"Are you sure that you can continue in this blinding place?" Myrddin asked.

"Of course," Benja said, without hesitation. "If I left you alone, you'd probably get yourselves eaten in the first few hours."

Myrddin laughed again.

"Well then," he said, "let's move. We still have a lot of ground to cover before nightfall."

They all rose and shook themselves off. Myrddin, Droran, and Ava had taken several steps forward when they noticed Benja stood frozen, cocking his head to one side.

Myrddin cocked his head too, listening carefully. But he could make nothing out. He looked at the little mole expectantly.

"What's going on?" Droran bellowed.

"Hush!" Ava commanded, shoving his shoulder. They all turned and stared at Benja in silence until he spoke.

"I hear a drone, or something like it, and the inner workings of a robot, too. But nothing is touching the ground anywhere near here."

Myrddin shook his head with a smile of admiration. He had not realized that Benja could hear the inner workings of the machines.

"How far away are they?" he whispered.

Benja stared at his surroundings a little longer before begrudgingly admitting, "I don't know. It's difficult for me to tell in the open. I have no frame of reference to judge by."

The prince nodded for a moment before closing his eyes and reaching out with his magic. His eyes shot wide open in terror almost immediately.

"Run," he shouted. "They're... They're right under us!"

As the elf spoke, a squadron of drones shot up from the hole they had just exited. They hovered above the hole, guarding it, as a larger drone appeared, lifting a human-shaped robot out of the hole and depositing it onto the ground with a heavy thud.

As the group ran, the prince glanced back to see that drone-borne robots were emerging from the hole at an alarming rate. Each settled on the ground, paused for a second to orient itself, then started marching toward the prince and his friends.

The elf, dwarf, human and MoleKind scattered in different directions as they ran, trying to make the best pace they could to gain distance from the walking robots, but also using the trees as cover from the drones.

Their lungs were burning, and their legs ached. The drones chased them directly away from the hole, firing their light rays, which cut through the trees and scorched the ground behind their feet. They heard the pounding of the robot's boots, starting slowly, but now picking up speed.

As more machines emerged from the hole, the breathing party's slim advantages decreased even more. The marching robots drove them from behind and the drones flanked them from the sides and above, corralling the party into an open glade.

As they emerged into the glade, Droran tripped on a root and lost his balance. As he rolled to regain his footing, a single drone made a dive for him, sliding its laser guns inside its body and extending one of its sharp propeller blades to the front, ready to shred the dwarf into slivers.

Benja had been running ahead of Droran and turned to see his distress. He rushed toward the dwarf, and as the drone passed over his head, he jumped up and swiped at the flying menace with his claws to deflect the spinning blades. He scraped the side of the drone and deflected its path slightly, so it barely missed the struggling dwarf. But it wasn't damaged. The drone rose and reformed with its squadron, as if discerning the next opportunity to strike.

Myrddin could not pay much more attention to Droran's plight, as he was raising his sword to block the scissoring blades of the robot in front of him. A continuous clang rang through the air as the blades pounded relentlessly against his sword. He was certain that, had his blade not been so heavily enchanted, the robot would have destroyed it with its first contact.

As the robot was focused on Myrddin, Ava powered up her own weapon and thrusted it into the back of the robot's neck, creating an ear-piercing grinding noise. Its head shuddered back and forth on its neck springs. When Ava severed those, the head shot off like a stone from a sling, barely missing Myrddin as it spun away.

Ava and Myrddin dove for the treeline as the robot's body landed with a thump where they had just been standing. Drones that had been aiming for Ava missed their target and sliced the robot into several sections, cutting off both arms and one of its metal boots. The drones ceased their fire and regrouped.

From the cover of the treeline, Myrddin and Ava watched as Droran, now recovered and filled with Dwarven battle-rage, dove for the severed robot boot. He inspected it for a second, smiled, raised it over his head like a hammer, and charged the nearest robot with an impressive battle cry.

Myrddin almost chuckled. Droran caught the robot in the knees from behind and the metal beast tumbled to the ground. But before anyone could celebrate the victory, drones circled him with fire as the robot rose and shook itself off. It swung a bladed arm at the dwarf, and he instinctively blocked with his own arm. The blade did minimal damage, as Droran finally experienced firsthand just how thick his skin was. The force of the attack though, threw him some distance as if he weighed no more than Benja.

A squadron of four drones all dove for Benja, who stood with his claws ready to fight. The drones extended their cutting blades and formed into a V formation. Even if the first drone was destroyed, one of more of the others would finish the job.

Without thinking, Myrddin stretched out his hand and uttered an elven incantation, hoping to use his magic to push the drones off course, giving the mole time to escape. As he pulled his concentration inward, he involuntarily sensed a powerful magical presence in close proximity. That presence being so intense, and so close, it intruded upon his inner senses. With no idea who or what this creature was, and possibly without even consciously intending to do so, he cried out to the presence, begging whomever or whatever it was for help.

It responded instantly.

A deafening roar echoed through the air above them. Benja felt the fur on the top of his head being singed with heat as a stream of orange flame poured down upon the diving drones. He ducked and rolled to the side as the drones, and the flames, hurtled in his direction.

Myrddin and Ava stared in amazement as the mole scampered into the treeline and the squadron of drones melted in midair, splattering like a pile of steaming silvery mud right where Benja had been standing seconds before.

When they lifted their heads to get a better look at their unknown ally, they both froze in amazement.

The creature's blood red scales were tinted with speckles of gold on the very ends, reflecting light in a way which made it sparkle like a glittering ruby in the sky. His wings now flapped furiously to slow him from the dive he had been making to save Benja. The wind nearly knocked Ava and Myrddin to the ground.

It was not as big as the dragon Myrddin had seen in his first encounter with the machine army. More the size of a house than a mountain, but still impressive.

Benja's would-be killers were nothing more than a pile of melted metal. The stench of the burning plastic and rubber that filled the air made Myrddin want to retch.

The dragon swooped up above the trees and entered aerial combat with the three remaining squadrons of drones. He took out the first group easily with one continuous stream of flame. But the other drone groups appeared to have had time to recover and strategize. They separated far apart and advanced on the dragon, alternately firing at him from opposite directions, and then ducking away as he turned toward them.

On the ground, the prince's blade slashed through the neck of another robot, sending a surge of electricity through his arms.

The dwarf was contending with a robot head on, bashing the boot against the robots spinning blades. Myrddin saw the robot step back and open its cannon compartment, like the dwarf in his dream.

"Droran! Watch out!" He cried.

The projectile launched, but Droran spun to his side to avoid it. It barely missed him and exploded when it hit a tree.

As Droran recovered, Benja finished the robot with a single, strategic sweep of his claws. Ava and Myrddin took down two more, either by Ava dismembering them while Myrddin distracted them, or by distracting them herself while Myrddin took them down with his sword.

Now that the dragon was occupying the overhead threat, Droran, Myrddin, and Ava moved to the center of the clearing together, backs facing each other, weapons extended, ready to protect each other. They looked up and stared as the drone squadrons pecked away at the dragon, and he screeched and spewed fire at them in return. The aerial battle was at an impasse.

They had barely a second to wonder if they could somehow help their flying comrade, before their own peril again commanded their full attention. Six walking robots emerged from the treeline in all directions, surrounding them. They marched slowly toward the party, each extending their bladed arms.

Myrddin sized up the situation and did not like the odds. They were outnumbered two to one and they could not use their "distract and attack" technique as before. Plus, they were surrounded.

He looked around for Benja but did not see him. Had he been killed in the woods? The prince hoped perhaps he had escaped, maybe to find help. Hopefully, at least he would live to fight another day.

The robots inched closer to the group, now holding their blade arms out to their sides, creating a circle of death in case any of the breathing creatures tried to run. When their blade arms were almost touching, and they were just a few steps from the party, they stopped walking and slowly turned the spinning blades toward the warriors.

Myrddin, Ava, and Droran all glanced at each other and nodded. They were ready to take out as many of these accursed monsters as possible as they made their final stand. But as they raised their weapons, the ground beneath them began to rumble. They looked up and down in confusion, as did their attackers. Ava gasped as the robot standing in front of her wobbled, unsteady on its feet.

Then, the ground beneath the metal beast simply opened up and swallowed it.

The remaining robots stood, looking from side to side, as each one of them disappeared into the ground and dropped out of sight. The team could feel heavy thuds beneath them as the robots crashed somewhere far below.

The elf, dwarf, and human stood in the middle of the empty glade, surrounded by six perfectly round holes.

Their confusion was interrupted by a blast of wind from above. The dragon was diving toward them at a frightening speed. The two squadrons of drones converged to keep up. As the mighty creature neared the ground, he extended his bleeding wings wide and swooped upward so quickly one of the lead drones crashed into the ground not far from Droran.

As the dwarf finished the crippled drone off with his boot, the other machines recovered and followed the dragon into the sky. He spun his body and extended his wings, holding himself in midair for a second. They were gaining on him, and their beams stung his outstretched wings. But now they had drawn together in a single V formation to catch up with the dragon during his rapid descent.

Just like the dragon had planned.

He spewed out a furious flood of heat, spraying enchanted flames across the double-squadron of drones. The high-pitched whine of their rotors sputtered, quieted, lowered in pitch, and then stopped altogether as they melted and descended. Their remains landed in a small pond, which erupted with steam, then absorbed them as if they had never existed.

The dragon made a large circle in the air, presumably checking for any more threats. As he did, the rest of the team looked back at all of the holes. Droran was peering down into one of them when Benja's head popped out of it, startling the dwarf so badly he fell backwards to the ground.

They all laughed and helped both Benja and Droran to their feet.

"Nice work, my friend!" Myrddin exclaimed, clapping Benja on the shoulder. Then turning he said, "Nice work, all of you."

As they congratulated each other and surveyed their surroundings, they looked up to see the dragon, who landed effortlessly beside them.

"Greetings, great one," Myrddin said immediately, falling to one knee.

The others followed his lead and did the same.

At first, he thought the dragon would not speak, but then he felt something brush through his mind, speaking to him in a language which had been dead for a long time.

"Greetings, Myrddin of the Elves, Ava of the Humans, Droran of the Dwarves, and Benja of the MoleKind. I am Pyrrhus of the Dragons."

The expression on the creature's face had not changed at all, and there was no sign that he had spoken.

"Greetings, great Pyrrhus. We are thankful for your help. Without you, we would surely have perished," Myrddin spoke aloud, with his head bowed. He had heard, or perhaps read, that dragons were accustomed to being treated with respect, and he did not want to offend their benefactor. "It is especially appreciated since I've heard dragons seldom involve themselves in the affairs of other races."

The young dragon spoke into Myrddin's mind. "The dragon emperors and senate have decided that ground races are a lost cause."

Myrddin looked at those around him. They appeared to hear the dragon too, or at least their glazed eyes seemed to indicate it. He hoped they were also able to feel what he was feeling. The sense of kindness, of integrity. This dragon spoke the truth.

"How will you assist us if your elders disapprove?" Myrddin asked. He knew the political power in the dragon empire was primarily based on size and physical prowess. If that was true, then this creature in front of him would have be in grave danger if they found out he was helping them.

"I will return as I can." Pyrrhus said simply, "This will help you to contact me." He said as he touched his snout against the prince's forehead.

The prince's body jolted, and he swayed on his feet as if struck by a hammer. He grabbed onto the dragon's head to steady himself. Pyrrhus stood like stone with his eyes closed, not reacting to the prince's movements or touch.

Slowly, Myrddin's mind opened to the mind of the dragon. The sensation began similarly to when he would reach out and see things with his magical inner vision. But in this case, he saw memories as if they were his own. He remembered thoughts and feelings, conversations, and events as if he had experienced them himself.

The sensation began to overwhelm him, and his body began shaking again. Pyrrhus sensed this and pulled his mind back a measure, allowing the prince to adapt to the new experience. Myrddin's breathing began to slow and his mind explored the new thoughts and memories.

The prince saw, or rather experienced, the fury that filled the dragons. It was a seething rage which permeated their souls. A rage at the injustice of what was lost since the Great Change. A rage at how their world was being destroyed. A rage at how their once elegant race and culture had deteriorated into a military state whose only goal was survival.

But shining through the anger, Myrddin also felt the compassion and conviction of the massive creature he was now leaning on. He felt the agony Pyrrhus felt as he "remembered" seeing ground dwellers being slaughtered in battle and the frustration being blocked from helping them.

The intense feelings from the heart of the mighty beast overwhelmed him again. He released his hold on the dragon's nose and fell backward.

When he woke, the others were hovering over him with concerned faces. The dragon was gone. For a moment Myrddin wondered if the entire experience of meeting a dragon had been one of his dreams. But he looked around at the piles of melted and smoldering metal and confirmed that it was real.

They stared at each other for a beat, then Droran burst out laughing, breaking the silence.

"Well, that's not something you see every day," he chortled, throwing the robot foot into the air before catching it again. He turned to Ava, her helmet's visor closed firmly, and only a few dents visible in the armor. "I see now why you wear this stuff. Very solid."

"Come on," Myrddin said, shaking his head clear of thoughts, and getting back on track. "We need to get going. We still have a mission to complete."

Chapter 15

Myrddin surveyed their surroundings to gather his bearings. Towards the outskirts of the meadow, he saw the colorful wildflowers he had smelled earlier. Bees were buzzing around them, collecting nectar, while butterflies flitted through the tall stalks. He reached out with his inner sense to scan for threats. For the first time in his travels, all he sensed was nature as it should be; trees, grasses, animals, and the radiant magic of the world itself. Even the spirits of his comrades, while serious, were filled with hope and possibility.

Never had something so simple been so beautiful before.

They made good time once they exited the meadow, for which he was grateful. They all seemed to have renewed vigor in them. The fresh air and sunlight, having defeated the squad of robots and making a new ally all boosted their morale. Although he regretted the trees thickening and blocking the light, he was thankful Benja would not have to struggle so much with the brightness. All in all, they were doing well.

The landscape gradually transformed. They passed through thick clusters of trees where they had to walk in single file, following animal paths. Then they would emerge into clearings where they could spread out, but overall the forest was continually thickening, which meant they were getting closer and closer to centaur territory.

In one clearing, where a distant mountain peak was visible above the foliage, he pulled out Bayard Andorris's maps and pinpointed their exact location based on the location of the sun and other landmarks.

As they forged ahead, trees and brush became thicker yet. They wrestled through heavy shrubbery which Myrddin and Ava had to clear away with his sword and her spinning blade. The foliage eventually thickened to the point where they could barely move.

"These centaurs really have a great outer perimeter to defend themselves." Ava remarked.

"Aye." replied Droran. "No wonder so few have ever come back from these parts."

As they were approaching the limits of frustration, they came across something that distracted them from the foliage entirely. The prince held up his hand, stopping those behind him, before creeping close enough to touch it.

At first glance, the object before them appeared to be nothing more than a large pile of moss and vines, strewn over a massive rock, but it was a shape he had studied before. A shape which was definitely not that of a rock.

It was an ancient human automobile. A large metal chamber with four wheels which spun, allowing the humans within to be shuttled wherever they were going at great speeds. After the Great Change, they had all but disappeared as the machines had started pulling them apart for extra materials from which they could build more like themselves, or adapted to make autonomous, four-wheeled weapons.

This one had obviously not been touched in a long time and had almost become one with nature.

He explained to the others what it was, as he tore some the moss and leaves off the top, revealing the now red and rusty metal below which had probably been feeding the soil for centuries. He wondered if this was the vehicle Mythriya had used. It had been rumored, although no records were present and nothing had ever been confirmed from an eyewitness, that the last time she had left the Elven kingdom, she had been in one of these.

"Do you think we could get it working again?" Droran asked excitedly, the idea of going at great speeds obviously appealing to him.

"Even if we could, I doubt it would be of much use," Ava said, looking at the forest around them. "I think the only reason the other machines haven't cannibalized it is because it's stuck here."

Myrddin noticed how the inflated wheels which were supposed to grip the ground and propel the vehicle forward had deflated some time ago. On closer inspection, he observed each wheel had a gash, as if from a blade.

"I think the centaurs might have had a hand in that," Benja commented, staring at the wheel next to him, and speaking the words which had been in Myrddin's mind.

"This is not centaur territory, nor was it ever," the prince said thoughtfully. "They must have known it was here and came specifically to do this before the Great Change, or perhaps right after."

"So you are saying the centaurs have been here, and could return here again if they wanted to come and see us specifically?" Ava asked, or rather stated thoughtfully.

"I suppose so..." he trailed off.

They were fairly close to the centaur territory now, less than a five-minute human walk away, and the centaurs would likely have sentries placed on the border of their land. Perhaps even scouts this far out and further. They were by no means safe, but as long as they did not show any signs of progressing further into the centaur territory, then they should be fine.

"We'll camp here tonight, and decide on a plan in the morning," he said. "The brush is too thick to make a fire, plus we don't want to attract attention. So do what you can to get comfortable and rest."

"If we don't get our throats slit in the middle of the night." Ava quipped, sliding her helmet over her head and curling up in a patch of grass.

"I find the heather quite comfortable." Replied Benja, who curled up into a ball and tucked himself so far under a shrubbery he disappeared from sight.

"I'm not so tired. I'll stand the first watch." Offered Benja.

"Fair enough." Said the prince. "Wake me if you need relief."

"Aye my prince!" He said with a bow and a crisp dwarven salute. "But by your leave, I should prefer to wake lady Ava and give you your rest."

Ava grunted and waved her hand in agreement, and it was settled.

Myrddin marveled at the stamina of the little dwarf. His first reaction was to deny Droran's request, but part of leading was delegating and allowing others to do their part, so he agreed.

He focused his healing magic on his wounds for a few minutes. His ribs had not shifted and the new bone was firm. His skin and muscles were strengthening on both his hands and his side. The encounter with the rope vine and the battle with the robots had reversed much of the progress his hands had made in the mole hovel, but with some additional healing, he hoped to be battle ready before he encountered any more machines.

He finally fell asleep, but unlike the peaceful sleep of those around him, it was a pitiful rest, filled with troubling dreams he could not remember when morning came. He woke up more tired than he had been the night before..

Even though he was not nearly as rested as he would have hoped, the rays of the sun were still as energizing as they had been when he had first seen them the day before. He enjoyed their warmth so much he wondered how he had survived so many days in the caves without it.

His friends were still sleeping behind him and he decided not to disturb them. Instead, he wandered a short distance from them and alternated between sharpening his sword and focusing this magic on his wounds.

Finally, his companions awoke. They all took a light breakfast from their provisions and set out.

As he had estimated the night before, they were about to pass into centaur territory. His feet crunched on something suddenly, causing him to look down at it. He was unsure at first of what the pale white item was, but as he dug at the surrounding ground, he recognized the item instantly. It was difficult to mistake a skull, though he wasn't sure if it had belonged to a human or a dwarf.

"You think that's recent?" Droran asked.

"It depends on your definition of recent," the prince said, looking at the slightly yellowed bone. There were still bits of flesh at the edges. "No more than a few months," he answered.

"That's a bit too recent for my liking," the dwarf replied. Myrddin nodded his head in agreement.

The prince was surprised they were not attacked or challenged as they entered the centaur lands. From what he knew of the centaurs, it was highly unusual. He would have expected to have been stopped before he had put so much as a foot into their territory. They occasionally saw hoof prints on the ground too, and fresh ones at that, so it was unlikely their presence had gone unnoticed. While Benja and Myrddin both slipped through the forest silently, the stocky dwarf and the armored woman weren't exactly stealthy as they tramped through the brush.

Was it possible they were just extremely lucky? He doubted it.

A soft sound caught Myrddin's attention. The noise was so slight he had probably been hearing it for some time but mistaking it for the wind in the leaves. He held up his hand to stop the group. He silently cupped a hand to his ear and nodded at Benja. Benja returned the nod and closed his eyes, whiskers twitching. He opened his eyes and took the lead position, listening and sniffing.

They all slowly followed the sound as silently as possible, using Benja's increased hearing to make sure they were going the correct way when the wind picked up and made it difficult to hear. But eventually the sound grew louder and louder until even Droran and Ava heard it clearly.

When they found the origin of the sound, the sight took their breath away.

There, amid a small clearing, was a lagoon with water as clear and blue as the sky on a cloudless day. Looking in, the group saw the pebbles on the bottom as if they were looking through a pane of blue glass. There was not a single sign of the sand at the bottom being disturbed, and not a bit of cloudiness in the water itself.

The sound they had been hearing had been coming from the waterfall which fell from the cliff at one side of the clearing, clattering onto the rocks beneath it before tumbling into the lagoon.

The entire scene struck them as unreal. The sun reflecting off the water and filtering through the trees was breathtaking. He was ready to jump into the pool, washing his body of the sweat and dirt which had accumulated over the past few days. That imagination was powerfully tempting. The thought of dropping his sword and diving, unarmed a vulnerable, into the water filled his mind.

He snapped out of the reverie and shook himself. Was this some kind of enchanted centaur trap?

"We are in the right place, aren't we?" the dwarf asked, looking around, confused.

"Definitely," said Myrddin, the scent of horse now clear in the air, and a few footprints visible in the sandy beach of the lagoon.

"Where are they all?" Ava whispered.

"What do you think, Benja?" the prince asked. "Can you feel any vibrations in the ground or hear anything we can't?"

The little creature concentrated for a moment before replying. "It has been the oddest thing..." he muttered. "I have been feeling the vibrations all over the place, and I keep hearing them. But we never run into them."

"Are they watching us?" Ava questioned. She sounded slightly insulted. "If so, what reason do they have to avoid us?"

"No," said Benja. "They are too far away to be watching us. It's as if they know exactly where we are going to be and when we are going to be there, and they have been staying out of our way."

"Hmm," Myrddin said as he pondered what the little creature might mean. The centaurs could see the future. Were they doing all of this on purpose?

"Um..." Benja started suddenly, but it was already too late. While they had been distracted, pondering the reason the centaurs had not attacked already. A troop of centaurs had surrounded them, moving more silently than Myrddin imagined creatures of their size would be able to. They towered over the elf.

His hand instinctively dropped to the hilt of his sword but froze. It wouldn't do much good at this point anyway.

The centaurs moved in on them before he could say another word. He heard Ava's cry as she was disarmed and pushed to the ground by a large centaur. This was immediately followed by the bellow of the dwarf as a centaur reared up and kicked away the boot hammer with blinding speed.

At these sounds, he could not stop himself from drawing his sword. But with a single flick of its spear, a pale, cream furred centaur flung the weapon away, into the hands of another centaur who snatched it expectantly, as if they were playing a game of catch.

He looked around at their situation and suddenly realized how strategic the movements of the centaurs had been. They were rumored to fierce and brutish warriors, but these creatures had waited patiently to ambush them and had done so as a single unit, making sure they disarmed everyone who had a weapon before they could use them. They already had an advantage from their size and surprise, but now they had the added advantage of being the only ones with sharp, pointy objects.

Fortunately, Myrddin knew he was not entirely unarmed. He had his magic, and his dagger was still in his boot, biting into his heel. He was already planning on how he could use the two to his advantage when he heard Ava shouting for him.

That was odd, he thought. He was sure the centaur had disarmed her, and she expected her to be dead by now, with him soon following. But she was not.

Listening carefully, and reaching out with his magic, he realized none of his companions had been harmed. They were simply being held back by some centaurs, being kept away from him and the creature in front of him who was simply observing him.

"Greetings, Myrddin of the elves, brother to the centaurs," the large centaur before him finally spoke. "We have been waiting for you for quite some time. Please follow me."

The spear was removed from his neck as the cream-colored centaur, obviously in charge, turned and showed for him to follow.

He looked around at his companions, who were as confused and overwhelmed by the situation as he was. So, he followed. Not that he had a choice.

Behind him, he heard the clang of steel striking steel. He swung around to see what had happened.

The two other centaurs had swung their spears down, meeting in the middle. Although he was grateful the sound had not involved one of his companions' blades and no altercation had occurred, it was clear that his companions were now completely blocked off from him.

"What is the meaning of this?" he asked the centaur who had given him permission to follow him.

"The invitation extends only to you, Prince Myrddin," the creature said calmly, glaring at the others in disgust. "It is only you who is our brother."

A shiver crawled down Myrddin's spine. He understood the unspoken message. Although Myrddin was relatively safe with the surrounding centaurs, his friends were not. And if it were up to the centaur in front of him, they would already have been slain.

He looked back at his friends, deciding whether it would be worth it to consider risking their lives by asking them to stay simply so he might feel more comfortable. Seeing the blood lust in the two guards, his mind was quickly made up. They would die the moment he was out of sight.

"I'll meet you all by the old vehicle. Maybe we can use it to salvage some parts for weapons." He looked at the dwarf and the MoleKind. "See what you can do."

They all fidgeted, to be hesitant to leave.

His eyes met Benja's. The wise MoleKind appeared to be the only one discerning the situation, rather than grumbling about being left out. The prince flicked his eyes up to the centaurs, and the little creature followed his line of vision.

Benja nodded. He was the only one among them who understood the violent and volatile nature of the centaurs. He knew they were in great danger and getting out of their area was their best hope for survival.

"We'll meet you there, but if you aren't back by midday tomorrow, then we will be obligated to come looking for you." Benja replied with a grave tone.

The warning in the creature's voice was clear. He could not prevent the others from coming back for him. They would walk right into their deaths if he did not get back to them quickly enough.

Glancing at the sun, he saw Benja had given him roughly a full day. He hoped that would be enough.

"Very well. I'll meet you back at the vehicle no later than noon tomorrow."

Ava in particular looked like she was going to complain, but Benja reached up to her, placing his hand on her shoulder to get her attention and shaking his head. The prince made sure he did not take his eyes off them until they had faded from sight.

He turned to the centaur in front of him, who also appeared to have calmed a great deal now they were no longer in the presence of the other races.

"Lead the way," he said, nodding his head.

The centaur walked towards the waterfall, before ducking his head and stepping right through it.

Myrddin looked around in surprise. He could see nothing on the other side of the waterfall, even now that he knew there must be a passage there. He took a deep breath and stepped blindly into the cascading stream.

The cold water rushed over him, washing away some of the dirt which was caked onto him. He was so refreshed by the icy water he actually delayed his exit for a second, just standing there, and allowing himself to be cleaned before he emerged on the other side. When he did so, what he saw, and what he felt, shocked him.

He was no longer in the forest.

Instead, he was standing at the bottom of a rocky canyon. Red and brown stone of various shades ran horizontally for as far as he could see. Looking up, he was almost blinded by the sun. It was high in the sky, uninterrupted by any clouds or any signs of vegetation. At the bottom of the canyon, where they were standing, he would have expected to see the large river which would have taken hundreds of thousands of years to cut through the stone so much, but there was only a small trickle of water, no wider than his forearm, and about as deep.

But what surprised him more than his location was the sudden change in his own body. Instead of being drenched in the icy water, he was suddenly perfectly dry and covered in what felt like a smothering blanket of hot, dry air, which almost choked him.

Glancing around further, he saw the centaur who had gone in before him standing, waiting. It was perfectly dry as well, and if he had not known any better, he would have thought nothing had happened. But, behind him, he could still see a small trickle of water, running down from the top of the canyon wall, spilling over a rock to create a thin stream, just wide enough and continuous enough for him to have been able to step through it like a curtain.

The centaur, who had been gracious enough to afford him a few moments to gather his bearing spoke, his voice echoing strangely between the stone walls.

"We need to move along," he said, although the prince barely made out what he said as it bounced backwards and forwards several times. "He is expecting you."

The prince wondered exactly what was meant by that. Who was expecting him? He could think of only one creature would know of his coming, the great seer of time. He had been certainly been invited, and his greeting so far, while brusque, was absolutely cordial for centaurs. But did that mean enough to afford him a meeting with the greatest of them, who had not been seen by any creature other than the centaurs themselves in more than a thousand years?

They stepped quickly, or at least Myrddin did. The elf was accustomed to being the swiftest member of his party, but compared to a centaur, he was as slow as a dwarf toddler. He resisted the urge to laugh at the situation. Was this how humans felt when they walked next to the elves? Had he been leisurely walking while Ava struggled to keep up, running along behind him without him taking notice of it?

The sound of their feet clopping on the stone ground confused him. He had never really realized how much he relied on his hearing while he walked. The sounds echoed backward and forward and being thrown at him from all different directions with no discernible pattern as the curves in the canyon walls kept changing slightly and changing the speed of the echoes. He felt mesmerized and confused, almost dizzy.

This sensation was enhanced by the harsh sun beating down on him. Without the protection of the trees, there was nothing to stop it from scorching him through his thin clothing. The lack of vegetation in the canyon meant every surface appeared to reflect light at him, making him feel like a hare roasting on a spit over a campfire.

He wanted to complain to the centaur, or to at least ask how much the journey would be, but this might come as an insult or a sign of weakness, so he held his tongue. He finally noticed a dull spot ahead of them, just ahead of them. The sound did not echo out of there and was instead absorbed. He wondered if the heat was affecting his senses and he was becoming delirious.

He had heard stories of people who wandered in desert lands losing their minds and seeing visions just before they collapsed from exhaustion. He speculated perhaps this was all some kind of cruel trap. Had the centaurs just lured him and his friend here to destroy him, watching the Elf Prince go mad and die for their amusement?

He wasn't sure if what he saw next convinced him he was safe or confirmed he had finally gone insane.

It was an oasis at base of the canyon in the otherwise parched desert. Filled with trees, so dense that it reminded him of the forest again. It cast glorious shade over the dry ground, allowing it to keep some of the much-needed moisture that it could not otherwise keep in the heat of the scalding sun. Luscious vegetation grew on the floor as well. There were deep green ferns, thick, soft grasses and bright orange and purple flowers which swayed gently in the breeze.

It looked heavenly to him.

Reaching out with his magic, he saw the oasis was glowing brightly as well. This was a place of great magic. A holy place probably placed under the care of the centaurs by magic itself a centuries ago. He was honored to have been given the pleasure of knowing that places like this still existed, never mind the joy of actually being here.

As they approached, he realized he had been staring at more than plants. The creature in the center of the scene was saturated with so much magic he had initially blended in with the plants that surrounded him. The enormous centaur's coat was so dark he seemed to be but a shadow, absorbing the light around it as if he was absorbing the surrounding energy into himself.

He realized the other centaurs had stopped walking forward with him. The clattering of their hooves on the hard stone beneath their feet had stopped, and the only sound was that of the light breeze whistling through the canyon, and the barely discernible trickle of the little stream of water. He glanced back to see them paused, heads bowed at the creature before them.

Unsure of whether he should continue, he paused momentarily. The centaur that had spoken to him raised its head slightly and indicated for him to continue with a small wave of his hand, like one might encourage a child.

He turned back, feeling more hesitant than ever, but the sun above him was halfway into its descent and had touched the sides of the enormous walls which rose around them. He did not have time to waste. The lives of his companions depended on his ability to get this done as quickly as possible.

The moment he stepped onto the grass; he was overwhelmed by the sensation of calm. The shade covered him much like the water from the waterfall, sending a wave of coolness down his body. He resisted the urge to sigh with satisfaction after a hard few hours in the sun. He had not realized just much of a toll the trip had taken on his body until that moment.

His eyes, however, remained fixed upon the creature in front of him.

Chapter 16

Now that he was in the shade, he could see the dark creature much more clearly. It was definitely a centaur, and a regal-looking one at that. It was bent over a pool of water which formed where the stream collected before traveling further. The stream appeared to be the source of this oasis, both physically and magically.

As he approached, the centaur did not look up but continued to stare into the pool. His black hair loosely hung halfway down his human-like torso, obscuring his face. Myrddin paused again and waited.

The centaur spoke. His silky voice resembled his shadowy coat. It came from deep within and sizzled around the oasis in a way which seemed to energize the air, while simultaneously drawing energy out of it. Each word sent chills down the elf's spine as if he were standing in the middle of a lightning cloud. "Come and gaze into the pool, Myrddin of the Elves. Tell me what you see?"

Myrddin approached cautiously, standing on the opposite side of the pool. He examined the centaur carefully. From this angle, he could see its dark eyes as well, although they remained fastened upon the pool. He had heard tales about the ancient Seer of the Centaurs and expected him to be withered and grizzled. Perhaps the centaurs lived for far longer than the elves, or perhaps the magic of this place had preserved him.

"Are you Aldrich, Seer of the centaurs?" he asked quietly, unable to resist the urge to understand his surroundings.

"I am, young one," the centaur replied calmly. "Are you surprised it is I who called you here?"

Myrddin thought about it for a moment.

"I am not."

The centaur nodded approvingly. "Settle your mind. Gaze into the pool, and tell me what you see," the centaur said again, still not pulling its eyes away.

Myrddin stared into the pool, surprised he could not make out the bottom at all. Instead, the dark blue continued for an eternity, not interrupted by anything. The thick canopy above prevented even a hint of sunlight from disturbing the water, and the hot breeze had completely disappeared around him.

He stared intently, trying to find what the seer wanted him to, but nothing came up. It was just blue water, exactly as before.

"I see a deep pool," he said eventually. "It is dark blue and seems to be completely undisturbed..." he trailed off. Unsure if this was what the centaur wanted to hear from him.

It was not.

"Clear your mind of all things," the centaur said, still speaking as calmly as he did before. "Do not think of what I want to hear from you, or of what you should see. Only gaze... and be... nothing else. Then tell me what you see."

He squinted and stared harder. But nothing changed. He knew he had to be seeing something else, had to be seeing something significant, otherwise he would not have been brought all this way to stare into a pool. But what?

"Clear your mind," the centaur said again, still not showing a hint of impatience or frustration.

He closed his eyes for a moment, taking a deep breath. He tried to calm his racing thoughts and to clear his mind. Eventually, he thought back to his nights in the Elven castle. He felt a surprising desire to let his mind drift toward the dreams which usually troubled him. Dreams of battle, of his sister, of his mother. As he did so, he saw those dreams in a different light than he had before. Not as a painful curse, but as a magnificent gift. A gift which his world and his people needed, whether they appreciated it or not.

An overwhelming peace washed over him. His mind cleared. His anxious thoughts melted away like the drones under the breath of the dragon. He felt the clarity of his mind coming into sync with the clarity of the pool in front of him. When he was confident he could maintain a sense of "nothingness" in his mind, he opened his eyes and gazed into the pool.

The calmness of the pool drew him in as his mind seemed to merge with it. The water was so smooth, there was nothing to interrupt his thought. The color was so solid, with no noticeable variation to distract him. His physical vision, looking at the pool, merged with his magical inner sense, becoming one in a way he'd never experienced before.

Suddenly, the serenity of the pool was shattered by an overwhelming flood of sights, sounds, thoughts, and feelings. He was somewhere deep underground. It was darker than he had ever known anywhere to be; the air felt thick to him as he breathed, heavy and damp. And there was a clattering, like the walking of an Arachnid, only louder and more metallic.

A creature appeared from the darkness. It was illuminated clearly, but Myrddin could not discern any source of light around it. He could see only it, but nothing else. Its face was metal like the robots, but it held some humanoid features which the robots he'd battled did not have. It resembled drawings from elven libraries of the robots the humans owned before the Great Change, back when humans created robots with friendly humanoid faces to serve them in their households.

Then he saw the body of the monster. It was the opposite of amicable looking.

Its body had been contorted thousands of times with new pieces roughly welded and bolted on until it contained mismatched arms and legs of swords, spinning blades, swinging hammers, and a variety of other items. It was suited to kill and injure no matter which way it turned. It turned its head and stared directly at Myrddin, its glowing red eyes striking horror in his soul.

Thankfully, the vision of the horrendous creature faded, and instead, he was somewhere else, somewhere deeper. The air was thicker here, and so hot he thought he might catch on fire by simply being there. This place was not dark, though. Rather, it was filled with rivers of molten rock.

Under a waterfall of this molten rock, he saw another strange creature.

It had the frame of a dwarf, but it was covered in horrible burns which should have been impossible to survive, even for one of his race. Its hands, which reached into the fiery river without flinching, were crumpled in on themselves, the skin between the fingers melted together. It seemed like it would be difficult to use them, and yet the creature was clearly working on something.

Drawing it from the river of fire, the prince could only make out a jewel-encrusted handle before the images changed again.

This time, he was somewhere on the surface, the thin air giving it away almost instantly, although the sky was so dark it might as well have been underground. Nothing was living in that place, not even a root was left in the ground. Not even an old, moldy seed. There was only darkness and the robots.

In front of him was a collection of boxes made of a strange black substance. He had seen nothing like it before. The boxes appeared to be alive somehow. Slowly, uncontrollably, he reached out and placed his hand on the object. He regretted it instantly.

His mind was filled with thoughts of destruction and growth. This world did not suit him. The oxygen in the atmosphere smelled toxic and burned his skin. The creatures who breathed it were an infestation of troublesome insects who needed and deserved to be exterminated.

He needed to spread, make more room for his empire, an empire of perfection and peace. He felt a sense of calm satisfaction. He simply needed to wait for the metal coming in and he would be able to expand again. It was only a matter of time before he and his kind would shape the world into a paradise. The deep feeling of satisfaction at a world without breathing life shocked Myrddin at first, but as his mind coalesced with the mind of the beast it almost began to make sense to him.

The prince was pulled out of his vision by the feeling of his back hitting the hard earth beneath him.

He searched around, gasping, realizing he was still in the oasis, but he was no longer standing over the pool. Instead, he was lying flat on his back, the dampness from the ground beneath him seeping into his tunic, and Aldrich was standing over him.

He was surprised by the change in position and realized he must have either fallen over or been pushed by the centaur. The answer was given to him almost as soon as he had thought it.

"I would not have let you in if I was going to let you get lost."

The centaur had knocked him over and pulled him out of his trance.

"Thank you," he said immediately, standing as quickly as his shaky legs would allow him.

"What did you see?" the centaur asked again.

Myrddin realized if these were visions of the future, then Aldrich had probably seen them too, so he told him everything he could recall, without leaving out a single detail.

They stood for a moment; the centaur towering over him even though he was standing at full height before the creature nodded.

"You have done well," Aldrich said plainly. "It has been some time since one has been born with the skill to see what others can not. Your talent is strong."

He felt honored to be regarded as talented by the centaur, but he honestly did not know what he had done, or how he had done it. All he knew was that the pool had helped him in some strange way.

Suddenly, the centaur moved. It had been the first time that Myrddin had ever seen him doing so and it startled him. The creature radiated power both through his enormous size and crisply defined muscles, but also by the magic which radiated from him so intently the prince could not look at him directly for more than a second.

It walked further into the trees, nodding for the elf to follow, which he did. He was surprised when he was led to a set of blankets covered in food more supple and plentiful than he had ever seen before, not even in paintings of elven feasts of old. The variety of fruit, some of which he had never seen before overwhelmed him. Different types of bread and meats were arranged in an inviting and artistic display.

The centaur motioned for to him to sit, and he did so, his companion doing the same on the other side.

"Eat," the creature said bluntly, waving to the food before him. "Eat, and I will explain all."

The prince was hesitant, but did as he was told. He started with a single grape, which burst in his mouth, covering his tongue in a juice sweeter than any he had ever tasted before. When nothing ill happened to him, he picked up a small roll of bread with a square chunk of yellow cheese and consumed that as well.

He glanced up occasionally, between bites of his delicious meal, and observed the centaur. He too was eating, although not with as much gusto as the half-starved prince. And he paid Myrddin little attention. He appeared to prefer to stare straight ahead, his glassy eyes not appearing to focus on anything in particular.

Once Myrddin finished with his meal and unable to consume a single morsel more, that the centaur's eyes met his again, and the creature spoke.

"What you saw, I have seen as well," Aldrich began. "It was neither the future, nor the past, but rather the present elsewhere."

"The present elsewhere?" Myrddin asked, slightly confused.

Aldrich nodded. "It is the present. But the events were in another place. Several other places, to be exact."

The prince thought about the centaur's words, running them over in his head.

All of that truly happened. That creature, horrible and grotesque, actually existed somewhere. That dwarf did too, and whatever he was making. And finally, the strange collection of black boxes with thoughts of growth.

"What was that last thing?" he asked. It seemed to be the most important, and he could not get it out of his mind.

"That is the mother of all machines. If you were to compare them to a colony of bees, then the robots would all have different tasks - workers, warriors - but that creature would be the queen."

"It wants to kill us all," Myrddin said.

"It does," the centaur confirmed, giving a single nod of its head.

"Where do I need to go to stop it?" Myrddin asked. Now he had been inside the head of the thing, he had a renewed vigor for his cause. If what the seer said was right, he would have to hasten.

The centaur paused for a moment, staring into his eyes, analyzing. Myrddin felt uncomfortable and struggled to resist the urge to squirm. Just when he thought he could not stand it anymore, the creature turned his face away.

"You already know the answer to that question," he said flatly.

Myrddin would have liked to protest, but he knew better. He thought hard for a moment. Then, remembering his experience at the pool, closed his eyes and cleared his mind. He had been trained for many years how to reach into his inner, magical sense, but now he found he could go deeper, and more quickly than ever before. He hoped this ability would continue once he was outside this enchanted space.

That was when he saw the answer. It was simple.

Aldrich had mentioned how they were like bees. And there was only one sure way to stop an entire colony of bees.

"Kill the queen," he muttered.

The centaur nodded and said nothing more.

"Why did you invite me to this place? It was one thing to call me one of you because of the ability that I seem to have been born with," he said, having long since surmised there was nothing he had ever actually done to earn the ability to have his visions. "But why did you bring me into this sacred place? Why let me see into the pool?"

The centaur stared at the elf. On the surface, one might have described it as a blank stare. But the prince glimpsed an eternity of wisdom as he glanced back for a second, then averted his eyes.

"You have talent, but you are like a child; untrained. There can only be one great seer in every generation and when my time is up, it will be you who takes my place. You need to be trained."

"Trained?" asked the prince. He had been so used to people ignoring his ability for so long that the idea of actually receiving training in it sounded ridiculous.

"When having visions of the future in your dreams, you did not know how to direct them. Your mind was cleared but only partially, and so certain misconceptions took over. Do you not remember when you were battling the drone army? You were wearing the armor of a traditional Elven warrior in your dream. But in reality, you were wearing only what you have come to me with today."

The prince glanced down at his simple tunic, only changed for this meeting. He also recalled his dream. The centaur was right. But he had not finished.

"Likewise, when you used the pool to channel your ability, you did not know where to look, and so you looked at where magic was the most present or the most absent in the world. You did not direct your vision at all. Your control was so weak you almost allowed your mind to be consumed by the queen."

He struggled with the concept that he had been so close to danger without noticing it. He did not know going into the entire situation that there could be any threat posed to his safety. The idea of his utter ignorance gave him pause.

"I do not have time for extensive training," he said, frustrated beyond belief. He would have loved to stay for as long as possible and learn as much as he could, but he also understood he was not willing to sacrifice his friends out in the woods. Soon they would come storming in and likely be killed, thinking he was in danger.

"I am aware," the centaur said. "The others dislike the weaker races and find great displeasure with them being in our forest. We are to protect this place with our lives. He said, waving their surroundings.

That did not surprise Myrddin. If the elves had any place as powerful as this, with as much concentrated magic, then they would guard it with their lives as well.

"Just be aware that seeing beyond is not always as simple as it might seem," the centaur continued. "I grow tired of my role; it has been so many years I have been forced to isolate myself. I do not wish to have to wait another thousand years for one who is worthy to be born again."

His comment surprised Myrddin. From what he had understood, the role was a highly sought after one. The position of seer among the centaurs was akin to the position of a king amongst the others. But he understood at the same time. He had not wanted to be born into a position of power. He had not wanted to be the only heir of the elves. And position had indeed isolated him from others, but at least he still had other rulers he could relate to. The seers had no one else. By the time he was skilled enough to relate to the creature in front of him, it would probably be too late, and the centaur would pass on.

"I understand," he said. "I will be careful when I dabble with the art, but I will dabble and try to expand on my own. When this is all over, I will return to you."

He knew he could not resist, especially if the visions came to him in dreams again. How would he possibly be able to control something like that with the little experience he currently had? So he promised only what he could definitely complete.

The centaur nodded.

"It is rare to meet an honest creature in this corrupted world."

The prince smiled humbly and bowed his head.

"You must go now, young one," Aldrich said, standing suddenly. "If you wish to make it back to your friends before they are harmed, you will need to hurry."

Myrddin nodded, getting up without another word and walking in the direction that he knew would lead him out of the oasis.

He was surprised to find the sun had not only set while he had been in there, but had also started rising again. His perception of time in that sunless place of magic was completely skewed, and he suspected these visions had gone on for quite some time.

But, despite his lack of sleep and the overall excitement of the last few hours, he did not feel tired in the slightest. Instead, he felt more energized than he had been in his life.

Chapter 17

With the realization of the lost time, he started running through the canyons as quickly as he could. The more the sun rose the faster he could go. He saw no other centaurs in the area, having been left completely alone with Aldrich in the oasis. It was a strange experience to move so quickly on the firm stone without the clattering of hooves beside him.

By the time he reached the trickle of water, the sun had risen fully and was becoming visible above the walls of the canyon. The water appeared to be almost golden as it reflected the harsh light of the sun, and his mind flashed to the dwarf of his vision.

Aldrich had not mentioned him at all when they had been talking, but he did not appear to be surprised by his mention. The prince wondered about the significance of that place and the identity of the dwarf.

This time, the water left him damp as he jumped into the golden stream obviously had a solid stone wall behind it, and reappeared in the forest, jumping through the refreshing waterfall. He was glad for it though, as the sun had been quite intense without the respite of the oasis trees yet again.

Here he passed a centaur briefly, nodding to them as he passed and receiving a nod back. But he did not hesitate. He flew through the woods, energized by the respite with Aldrich, and his fear for the lives of his friends. He barely made it to the edge of the centaur territory before he saw the group marching in his direction.

"I'm here, I'm alright," he panted as he stood in front of them, struggling to remain upright with his lungs burning in his chest and stars appearing on the edges of his vision. His stomach rolled, threatening to spill the contents of the enriching meal he had eaten not too long ago.

His friends all beamed in relief that he was still alive, and the little dwarf even pulled him in for a manly hug.

"How was it?" asked Ava, eagerly, her face etched with concern.

"Interesting," he admitted between pants. "I'll tell you about it in a moment. First I want to get further away from the centaur territory, They don't like intruders, and that's what you are to them."

The dwarf nodded, grabbing the little MoleKind and ruffling the fur on top of his head.

"Oh, relax. It's not like it would be anything we couldn't handle."

Benja rolled his eyes at Myrddin, but he said nothing, simply walking in the opposite direction. Myrddin followed suit quickly and the human and dwarf did the same.

Neither the elf nor the MoleKind stopped until they had reached the human vehicle again.

Myrddin was surprised to see they had made a rather comfortable camp next to the relic and could even see the remains of the fire they must have made. He was pleased to smell the faintest remnants of a slightly charred rabbit too and was pleased he was not the only one who had managed to get something to eat. They would need their strength moving forward.

He sat down on the grass for a moment, looking up into the trees around them, thinking of the events which had passed and how he had yet again been lucky enough to save his friends in time. They all looked at him, waiting patiently. All except Doran.

"So, are you going to keep sitting there or are you going to tell us what happened after we left?" the dwarf asked gruffly, his impatience clear in his voice.

Myrddin could not help the little chuckle which escaped him at his companion's comment. He had to admit that for a few moments; he was afraid would never hear the sarcastic drawl ever again.

He thought through his words carefully for a moment, before settling with, "It was... interesting."

He could think of no better way to describe the experience.

"Interesting?" asked Ava. "I think that was a given." She laughed, along with the dwarf.

"Yes, I suppose it was," he said, cracking a smile of his own at how ridiculous his answer must have been to them.

"Did he help you find out where they were going next?" asked Benja.

"Not exactly," he answered, "but I do know exactly where we need to go to make the most difference in this battle."

The eyes of all of those around him grew wide.

"You mean there is something we can do about the situation?" Ava asked.

"There is," he nodded happily before his expression turned dark. "But it is going to be more dangerous than you could imagine. The likelihood of any of us surviving the journey is low."

"You mean more dangerous than all the situations we've been in already?" Ava laughed again. This time, even Benja chucked.

"I think even more dangerous," he said with a smile, "but I'm sure we will manage."

He only wished he felt as confident as his voice sounded. Myrddin was not his sister. He was not as strong, or as loved as she had been, but he had been given so much more responsibility than she had ever lived to see. He held the lives of all these people in front of him in his hands, and he could not make a single mistake.

"Of course, we will!" shouted Droran happily, as if it was the most obvious answer in the world.

He laid his eyes on Ava; he nodded at him warmly. And then he looked at Benja, who also nodded in confirmation. He was pleased he had found such loyal companions in such a shattered world.

He realized the one question he had forgotten to ask Aldrich when he was still there. Why?

He understood his natural-born talent had been the reason for them to invite him in as if he were one of their own, but he did not know why the centaur had directed him to the robot army. What had he seen in the future? What was the reason for everything?

He did not believe Aldrich would have done any of that if there had not been an important reason.

He was tempted to try and clear his mind, and find out for himself, but after his experience, he was not eager to go back into the visions again. It was too dangerous. Perhaps in the future, when he could return for his much-needed training, he would be able to ask the seer if he did not find out for himself.

Myrddin's mind drifted to the lone dwarf of his vision again. He could not get the creature out of his mind.

He had had so many questions answered that day, but questions had popped into his mind. He felt overwhelmed by his lack of knowledge, not used to it by any means. But he also understood he would have to get over that. He could not expect the world to be limited to what he knew, or expect himself to know of everything that happened in the world at all times; despite that being exactly what his father expected of him.

Shaking his head to bring himself back to the present, he started to explain what he had in mind, pulling out the maps which had been given by Bayard Andorris, what felt like a lifetime ago.

Under the expectant stare of the short-tempered human, the bull-headed dwarf, and the tiny MoleKind, he placed his finger on the map.

"This is where we need to go..."

THE END

Afterword

We hope you enjoyed the first story in the Dragons Vs. Drones saga, and that you will join us for the next tale, "Exile of the Dragon".

If you want to learn what REALLY happened during "The Great Change" and how the world of Alyrraesia looked before the machines took over, there's a novella called "The Great Change" that you can receive and read for free at this link.

https://www.brettmonk.com/community

When you join the community, you will not only get free books and other content by me and some of my friends, but you will get the inside scoop on discounted products and upcoming releases. Plus, I share some personal thoughts and "behind the scenes" photos and notes about my life, media adventures, and favorite grilling recipes. :-)

Community members also get to vote in polls and make suggestions for upcoming books and projects. You might even want to consider being a "beta reader" or an "advance review reader", both of whom get to read the books before they're available to the public!

More details are available at this link: https://www.brettmonk.com/community

About the Authors

Brett Monk Author Bio:

Brett grew up in the Shenandoah Valley of Virginia and got a degree in Radio / TV / Film in 1983. He has worked in the media for over 30 years. His experiences include directing live TV, industrial films, and feature length movies, including the "Mount Hideaway Mysteries" series of movies, which he directed and co-wrote. He was also a church-planting pastor for 10 years.

Brett originally got into writing as a screenwriter, and has since transitioned into focusing on novels and audiobook production. He enjoys collaborative writing and often works with a co-writer. He lives in Virginia with his family.

Lace Brunsden Author Bio:

Lace Brunsden was born in South Africa in 1998.

As a child she always had a love for writing, and often considered doing it professionally, but did not see it as a true career option, and therefore did not approach it immediately. Instead, she decided to attend the University of Pretoria, completing her Bachelor's degree in science, majoring in Biochemistry and Zoology, in 2019. However, her attention was quickly drawn back to writing, something that she had always loved.

Her first novel, a fantasy book for children, was published in July 2020.

Growing up in a Christian household, Lace had always been inspired by books such as The Chronicles of Narnia by C. S. Lewis, and she dreams of writing similar books and becoming a household name in Christian fantasy, especially for children. Her goal is to write many more books throughout the rest of her life; books that everyone can enjoy.

She leads a quiet life, on a large plot of land, with her husband Caleb and their dog Daisy, writing as often as she can.

www.ingramcontent.com/pod-product-compliance
Lightning Source LLC
Chambersburg PA
CBHW020333010826
48970CB00011B/649